RADIO BOY AND THE REVENGE OF GRANDAD

CHRISTIAN O'CONNELL

ILLUSTRATION BY Rob Biddulph

HarperCollins Children's Books

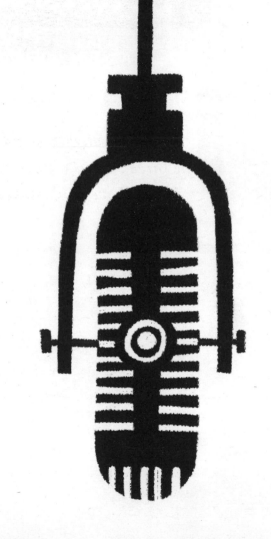

For Sarah, Ruby and Lois.
The three brightest stars in my world.
Love you, always.

Can you imagine what it would be like to have your very own radio show?

Just think about it for a moment.

You could do whatever you wanted, say what you wanted, and get your listeners to do ANYTHING.

Well, that's me. Spike Hughes. Living the dream. Surfing the radio airwaves from my garden shed at Number 27 Crow Crescent.

And the *Secret Shed Show* is live on air right now . . .

CHAPTER 1

the DJ who stole Christmas

'Spike, you cannot do this!' begged my radio-show producer, Holly.

'Oh yes, I can,' I replied.

The song came to an end. Time to speak. I suddenly remembered watching this old documentary with my dad about a motorcycle daredevil called Evel Knievel. He would jump over things on his motorbike. Cars, buses and planes. He even once tried to jump across thirteen London buses at Wembley Stadium. I felt like him, about to try to make that jump.

The MIC LIVE sign turned bright red, meaning we were on air. I spoke into the mic.

'So, who of you listening right now is brave enough to go and get one of your Christmas presents from under the tree, without anyone catching you, and open it up live on the show? Just grab one and call us right away!'

'This is a really bad idea,' said Artie, but I could see he was trying to swallow down his laughter as producer Holly scowled at us both.

A few months ago, after the whole school strike situation,* I had promised them both I would take it easy, but what's the point in having your own radio show if you can't have a bit of fun every once in a while?

I could see we had callers eager to take part in my 'bad idea'. I picked one.

'Hello, you're live on the *Secret Shed Show*. Who is this?'

'Hi, Radio Boy and the team.'

Artie and Holly mumbled back a very strained 'Hi', making it very clear they still didn't approve of what I was doing. Artie is my radio-show sidekick and he

---

* By situation, I mean masterminding a strike at school over crushing amounts of homework, which ended up with the headmaster breaking into my garden and having a tooth knocked out by Sensei Terry's front kick. That kind of situation.

also picks all the music. He doesn't really want to be a famous DJ like me. He's just here because he likes being part of it. Holly is my producer because she's the smartest out of the three of us. They are my best friends, and my only friends. I guess it's like being in a band together. Does that make Artie the triangle player?

Anyway, they knew all too well how much trouble could come from my spontaneous ideas. I'll tell you a little secret: this wasn't that spontaneous as I had planned to do it, but knew if I told them before the show they'd try to stop me.

'I've got a present to open from under the Christmas tree,' said our caller.

'OK. Firstly, what's your name?'

'Nick.'

'OK, Nick, describe the present to us.'

'It's huge, I can hardly lift it, almost the size of a door.'

'Is this your main present?' I asked. I was starting to get a little worried, as Christmas is all about the MP. The Main Present. Had Nick grabbed the big one from under his family's Christmas tree?

'Oh yes,' replied Nick. I could almost hear him frothing with excitement. You know what Christmas is like. It almost makes you sick with anticipation. It can't come soon enough. But for Nick, it would come right now, live, on my radio show. I looked at the terrified faces of Artie and Holly and hesitated for only a split second, then, excited by the power I had right at that moment, I shouted –

'Open it, Nick!'

Suddenly, the full horror of what I was doing got to Artie and he grabbed his mic, yelling:

'DON'T DO THIS, NICK! YOU'LL GET INTO HUGE TROUBLE!'

Holly's mouth was wide open, like she was watching a car crash in slow motion.

'DO IT, Nick!' I demanded.

He did it. We heard the unmistakable sound of wrapping paper being torn off – no, more *ripped apart* like a bear attacking a tent. There was no going back now. I had put tonight's radio show on a roller coaster. The question was, were we on the going-up bit, or plummeting down out of control?

Nick squealed in the most amazingly high-pitched way.

'OH WOW! OH WOW! OH WOW!'

'What is it, Nick?' yelled Artie. *Now* he wanted to play my game!

'It's . . . it's . . . it's . . . an Xbox, a brand-new Xbox,' said Nick, sounding as if he was crying with joy. The wonder of Christmas!

The moment was then shattered by the very loud footsteps we could hear from Nick's end of the line, and the sound of a door slamming open.

'WHAT ON EARTH ARE YOU DOING, NICK?' yelled a very angry-sounding man.

'R-R-R-R-Radio Boy made me do it,' stammered Nick.

Oh dear. Time for me to hang up quickly and play a song.

Then I remembered: Evel Knievel managed to clear all thirteen buses. But he crashed on landing. Breaking lots of bones.

Three Months Later

CHAPTER 2

Barbecued like a sausage

I suppose I should bring you up to speed with things.

The *Secret Shed Show* is still doing really well. Everyone now knows that I, Spike Hughes, am Radio Boy (which is kind of brilliant). At least people know I'm good at something other than being a total loser. It's official, I'm now 17 per cent less loser (not 20 per cent less,

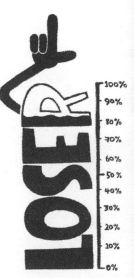

unfortunately, as my mum still insists on making me a packed lunch, whereas everyone else in my year just has the school dinners. '*Delicious fresh fruit to keep you regular, Spike, and gluten-free bread with nutritious mung beans, watercress and celery.*' If you want to know what this tastes like, try eating an old shoe with a dead toad inside it).

I always just quietly bin the leathery sandwich, and the dinner ladies give me a cooked lunch for free. I can see the pity in their eyes.

Being Radio Boy hasn't exactly changed my world *that* much, then. Let's look at the pros and cons of being a newly-fledged radio star in my world.

CONS:

Girls now officially find me funny BUT still just want to go out with the boys on the football A-team. I thought being 'school famous' would fix all this. Not so. Now I'm just their funny friend. A tap-dancing monkey is funny, but you don't want it to be your boyfriend.

To be honest, it's Artie that has been getting more of the attention from girls. They send him fan letters. He didn't seem that interested at first (or so he said), but I noticed he'd started putting gel in his hair and wearing his dad's aftershave. I say 'wearing'; I think it's fairer to say *it* wore *him*. Holly's and my eyes watered within a metre of him and his scent.

Even worse, Katherine Hamilton, the girl I once wanted to marry, is now going out with Martin Harris, the school bully and the son of my evil headmaster. I try to tell myself they deserve each other, but it's still like a stab to the heart whenever I see them together.

MORE CONS:

Our show would always be called the *Secret Shed Show,* but it wasn't really secret any more – and even though I still went by Radio Boy, I had lost my anonymity. This created problems. The biggest was, of course, my mum.

It started innocently enough, with occasional peering in through the shed window mid-show. Then it escalated to bursting into the shed studio while we were *doing* the show. Yeah, don't worry about the bright red glowing MIC LIVE sign, Mum. Just barge on in.

'There is a cold draught in here, I'll go and get your special jumper.'

'Are those electrical leads even safe? We had a poor young boy on my hospital ward just the other week who had been literally fried like an egg by faulty wiring. Poor kid had a permanent grin on his face. Even in his sleep.'

'Shall I make us all some nice soup?'

BTW:

My mum puts great faith in the restorative powers of soup. Like a simple bowl of soup is some highly potent ancient brew, not straight out of a can she just warmed up. My mum is a highly trained nurse, but her medicine cabinet appears to contain just three go-to things:

1. Soup.
2. Vicks VapoRub.
3. A cold flannel.

To my mum, this is the Holy Trinity of medicine. There is nothing that soup, Vicks or the application of a cold flannel cannot heal. If I was run over and lying in the road bleeding, my mum would go and get a stinking cold flannel and rub some Vicks on me before calling for an ambulance. By the time the ambulance had arrived she would have set up an IV drip, containing not blood, but chicken soup.

Anyway, my mum took to just bursting in on the show whenever she wanted.

So now there are two locks on the shed door. One on the outside to protect the broadcasting equipment from being stolen, and one on the inside to protect us from my mum.

'Spike, is this door locked? What if the fire brigade needed to come and rescue you as your studio turned into a human bonfire? Oh, my poor angel, barbecued like a sausage.'

My mum wasn't the only one trying to get in on the radio action, either. There was also Sensei Terry: our local postman, karate instructor and one-man neighbourhood watch. The man who rumbled the intruder in my garden, Fish Face, aka Mr Harris, my headmaster. Since then, Mum has given Sensei Terry permission to patrol our garden whenever he wants. It's not exactly like being given the freedom of the city, but in his mind it's *exactly* like being given the freedom of the city. The freedom to patrol at will in the garden of Number 27 Crow Crescent. The way he behaved, you'd have thought he'd caught the country's most wanted criminal.

Without warning, Sensei Terry will leap out of a hedge or from behind a bush and shout, 'Spike – all clear and safe!' and then disappear again. I'm sure I saw him last week disguised as a conifer tree following a suspicious-looking door-to-door salesman down the road.

EVEN MORE CONS:

Apparently everyone's a DJ. Who knew?

People at school keep giving me 'helpful' ideas of

exactly what I should do on the show and they are nearly always bad. Don't believe me? Here are some recent gems:

🎙 Matthew Howard in my year suggested I have a competition called 'Britain's Got Burps' to find the listener who can – well, can you guess? – burp the best. Thanks, Matt. Real classy.

🎙 Nan Fights. No, really. This came from Psycho Pete at school who even frightens the teachers. He's already about six foot tall and has a beard. At age thirteen. His dad, Psycho Pete Senior, is rumoured to be in prison. Psycho Pete Junior told me his nan could beat up anyone else's. I had no reason to doubt him.

🎙 Olivia Cooper in Year Eight

suggested: 'Which teacher would you like to see attacked by an animal and which animal?' Olivia is a nice girl, but she talks to an imaginary friend during the lunch break.

Radio gold, all of them. One day I might do an entire show full of these bad ideas. Get ready for Nan Fights Live!

On top of that, people also want to be on the show. I have a special way of dealing with this: Producer Holly. We have a system. I'm nice to people and say, 'I think you'd be great on the show – speak to Holly. She's the boss.' Then Holly will say to them very firmly, 'We aren't hiring right now. Ask again in a few months.' She does this in such a way that no one would ever dare ask again. It's in her eyes, I think.

I still feel anxious, though, anytime anyone wants to be my friend, or invites me over for a playdate. It's only a matter of time before I get hit with the 'I'd love to be on the show'.

HOLLY!

BUT OF COURSE THERE ARE ALSO PROS:

I'm starting to get free things. Yes, people send me *free* stuff in the hope that I'll talk about it on the radio show.

So far I've been sent:

 Ski boots from Snow Joke, the local ski shop. I've never been skiing and can't ski. Mum has given them to the local charity shop and they are in the front window next to an old wooden tennis racket and a wedding dress. The way they have positioned the boots, it looks like the wedding dress and ski boots are an outfit, ready to be sold to any passing ski-loving bride-to-be.

School shoes from Just Shooz. This is the new shoe shop in town, a bitter rival to Shoe City. I love the fact they called it Just Shooz. Like anyone has ever walked past a high-street shoe shop, seen all the endless rows of shoes in the window, and then wandered in and asked the helpful assistant where the pet dolphins are. 'Sorry, sir, "Just Shooz".'

Things are going so well, in fact, that just like an

actual proper radio station, we now have adverts. Well, one advert. It's for Mr Khan, the local newsagent.

He doesn't pay me in cash, however, as an advertiser normally would. Instead I'm allowed unlimited sweets, as is Holly. Sadly, due to Artie's very large sweet tooth (shall we say), he's had to have his offer limited to just one bag a week.

Mr Khan wrote the advert himself and I have to read it out twice during every show, complete with sound effects. He even has a big sign in his shop window that boasts, 'AS HEARD ON THE *SECRET SHED SHOW*'.

Here is my first-ever script for my first-ever advertiser:

SFX LARGE EXPLOSIONS
They have gone SWEET C-C-C-C-C-RAZY down at Mr Khan's!
SFX MORE EXPLOSIONS
This week Haribo Tangfastics are HALF PRICE! Hurry after school tomorrow before Mr Khan runs out!
SFX OF PEOPLE SCREAMING AND RUNNING
Also, why not check out Mr Khan's wide array of greeting cards for all occasions. Births, birthdays and

pet deaths. Yes! You heard us right, a sensitive card for someone special in your life who has lost their beloved pet. The PURR-fect idea!

Find it all at Mr Khan's Store. Penguin Parade, just opposite the dentist. No more than three schoolchildren allowed at any one time.

SFX MORE EXPLOSIONS

However, one thing hasn't changed – if anything, it's got even worse. And that's my relationship with my headmaster, Mr Harris.

CHAPTER 3

My headmaster hates me

I mean, I get it.

If I was in his shoes *I'd* hate me. I'd spend every waking hour thinking of new and ingenious ways to make my life hell.

I would never not be out of my mind if I was him.

My headmaster, Mr Harris, carries not just deep emotional scars from the showdown in my back garden, but also a very noticeable *physical* one. I mean *immediately* noticeable. Like, you wouldn't be able to stop looking at it if you were talking to him.

You see, Fish Face is now the only headmaster in the whole wide world with a golden front tooth. He had to have a new tooth to replace the one that to this day is still somewhere in my garden – knocked out with force by the legendary front karate kick of Sensei Terry.

Now, with his new golden tooth, Mr Harris's face looks even more evil. Like a James Bond baddie. Or maybe a *rejected* Bond baddie who was turned down for being too scary.

And that's unpleasant. But not as unpleasant as how Mr Harris must feel about it. I mean, I almost feel sorry for him. Every time he looks in the mirror he sees a reminder of what happened that fateful night in my garden. Marked for life.

Even worse, for months leading up to his manhunt for me, Radio Boy, I had made a laughing stock out of him on my secret radio show. To be fair, he started it. He launched the school's radio station, Merit Radio, and he should've had me on it – I mean, I was the only pupil at the school with radio experience (hospital radio; I was fired, but that's not the point). Instead, he put his idiot son, Martin Harris, on air and we became sworn enemies in that moment.

So, I mocked him mercilessly for weeks from my garden shed. I used a voice disguiser to mask my voice and real identity. I made up the name 'Fish Face' for him on air. He heard it. The school heard it. *Everyone* heard it. And when he finally tracked me down, Sensei Terry thought he was an intruder and knocked out his front tooth.

So it's not really *that* surprising my headmaster hates me.

Which was why I found myself staring once again at my own terrible reflection in the window at school.

'Do I *really* have to wear this?' I asked.

Fish Face grinned, his gold tooth glistening. He was grinning because my evil headmaster was successfully making my school life hell. It was payback. I was on litter duty again at lunchtime and he was making me wear a high-visibility jacket with the words 'RUBBISH COLLECTOR' printed on the back in large letters. The 'COLLECTOR' bit is microscopically minute. It reads like this:

RUBBISH
COLLECTOR

Oddly enough, I've never seen anyone else having to wear this particular design of vest.

'It's for health and safety, you see, Spike. I wouldn't want anything *unfortunate* to happen to you . . .' said Fish Face with fake sincerity as his fishy grin showed all his revolting coffee-stained teeth (and one golden one). Had he even been to a dentist this century?

If he ever *did* find a dentist unlucky enough to take him on, they'd need the industrial-strength jet washer to get those brown coffee stains off. And they'd need to have their own oxygen supply to protect themselves from his honking bad breath. Mr Harris can wilt flowers with just one small sigh.

No better way to spend your lunch break than wandering around your school in a high-vis jacket with a giant metal claw, picking up rubbish, as I did today. A constant soundtrack of 'Hey, you missed a bit!', as kids deliberately dumped sweet wrappers and crisp packets on the ground behind me. Let me say, for the record, it takes an awful lot of precision and skill to pick up a Curly Wurly wrapper with a giant metal claw.

Without realising, though, Mr Harris had actually done me a favour. At least, rubbish-collecting around the school grounds, I didn't have to listen to his lunchtime show on Merit Radio, which was blasted into every classroom and corridor. There was no escape – even in the toilets.

Things had changed on Merit Radio too. Before Mr Harris was arrested for breaking into my garden, the official school radio station had been presented by Martin Harris, with his dad barking orders in the background. Now Fish Face had decided to freshen things up and had put himself on air. This meant his son had a vastly reduced role. Martin had gone from presenting the show, to only speaking once an hour, with his new feature, *Martin's Minute*. In reality it lasted no longer than thirty-one seconds.

I *almost* felt sorry for him. But not quite. Once again, Fish Face was behaving like a wannabe dictator. In history we learned that some countries aren't like ours, and instead of an elected government, they have a 'dictator' who controls everything, even the radio and TV channels. They are only allowed to broadcast good news that's been approved by the mad leader. I think this was what Mr Harris had modelled Merit Radio on.

I'm pretty certain Mr Harris would be far happier running a small country like a crazy dictator. Banning things like jugglers, terrapins and the colour purple.

Anyway, back to *Martin's Minute*. This sound bite of radio gold had poor Harris Junior reading out official school 'good news' approved by his dad, to anyone unfortunate enough to be listening. All spoken like he had a gun to his head.

Merit Radio – more like Hostage FM. If this was on TV, Martin would be blinking 'free me' in Morse code.

'Good news . . . the leaking tap in the boys' toilets has been mended.'

Good news?! Only to plumbers and fans of all things tap-related. Back to Marty's minute.

'Further good news: the school cat is four years old today. If you see Cat, wish him happy birthday.'

That's not a spelling mistake, the school cat was actually called 'Cat'. It had been Fish Face's job to name it. Cat. Which sums up the man's creative powers.

Yes – it was *Martin's Minute*. But it felt more like *Martin's Endless Boredom Torture Hour*.

CHAPTER 4

The surprise house guest

'Grandad is here,' I shouted, after I spotted him coming down our front path after school. It was a cold March day and Grandad was about to brighten it up.

'What? Why? Oh no,' cried Dad in a horrified way. Dad is never very excited about seeing Grandad Ray, which I've always thought is odd. I mean, it's his own dad.

I opened the door excitedly and hugged Grandad.

'Spike!' he said in his typically booming voice. He

was wearing even more aftershave than Artie, as well as the big shiny gold necklace he always wore below his high, open lapels. I noticed he had two suitcases with him.

'Dad. What's going on?' came *my* dad's irritated voice from behind me.

'Well, I thought I'd come and stay for a few days. See my grandkids, help out around the house. That OK, son?' Grandad asked.

'Um . . . of course. Is Mum all right?' asked Dad suspiciously.

'Yeah, yeah, fine,' muttered Grandad Ray, pushing past him into the house.

Grandad Ray isn't like a normal grandad. Let me explain.

Firstly, the hair. It's not grey or white, like most men his age. It's white with a black stripe down the middle. It's also big. High and swept back. Never a hair out of place. It doesn't even look like human hair any more, after all the years of hair-spraying. It's actually a hair-based work of art. He always wears black cowboy boots too. No matter what the occasion. I think he even has cowboy-boot slippers. All of this would've looked perfectly normal if he was a part-time cabaret singer and ranch owner in Texas. Which he wasn't. Except he *was* a singer, of sorts – or had been – and in his mind he still is.

Grandad Ray used to be a cabaret singer on cruise ships, which is where he met Nan. His stage name was Toni Fandango. He quit dramatically after he was downgraded to performing on car ferries to France.

'I'm wasted trying to sing Frank Sinatra classics next to the fruit machines, Spike.'

Grandad blamed the end of his career on another, younger singer, Kriss Kristie. We all secretly knew, however, that it was due to his age and panda hair.

He opened his mouth and started to sing, right there in the front hall, at the top of his voice. He often broke into song without any warning.

'Youuuuuuuuuu ain't nothin' but a—'

Sherlock, my other best friend and full-time dog, immediately started barking.

'Bleedin' dog, shut it!' yelled Grandad.

'Ray, Ray, you sweet old man!' said Mum as she came rushing into the hallway.

'Here she is, greatest woman on Earth, what you saw in my son I'll never know,' Grandad said.

'How lovely of you to come and see us for a few days. Spike, take your grandad's bags,' ordered Mum.

I gladly obliged, but had a quick question.

'Um, where shall I take them?'

'To your room, of course, Spike. He can have your bed. You'll have to sleep on the inflatable mattress.' Awesome! Grandad Ray and I would be room-mates. Sure, it meant me having to sleep on the world's most uncomfortable bed, the dreaded inflatable mattress – like sleeping on a bouncy castle – but that was a small price to pay.

It took me two trips to lug Grandad Ray's suitcases upstairs. I passed Dad at one point and said, 'Look, snakeskin suitcases, proper showbiz.'

'Snakeskin! Fakeskin more like! The label on them says Poundland. Not sure a pound gets you a pair of authentic snakeskin suitcases.' They still looked very cool to me. At least no snakes had been harmed in the making of them. I'd love my boring school bag to be snakeskin like his suitcases. That'd soon catch Katherine Hamilton's eye.

'Oh, I love your bag, Spike; what's it made of?' she would coo.

'Python,' I'd say casually and saunter off.

'Here, you'll need this,' said Dad, snapping me out of my daydream as he threw me the foot pump for the blow-up bed.

CHAPTER 5

A new team member

'You owe me ten thousand pounds! Right NOW! Pay up! But . . . oh no . . . you don't have enough money, which means . . . I WIN!' yelled Grandad Ray as he cheerfully helped himself to me and my sister Amber's last bits of paper money on the Monopoly board.

Now he had bankrupted his grandchildren, Grandad Ray started doing a victory lap round the living room. He looked like a footballer who had just scored a hat-trick, trying to pull his shirt over his head – though his high hair got in the way.

'SUCKERS!! LOSERS! LOSERS!' he shouted while pointing at us. Grandad *really* likes to win. 'You snooze, you lose,' is just one of his supportive phrases.

Monopoly is without doubt the WORLD'S WORST GAME EVER. What a fun way to spend time, financially ruining your family members, taking all their money and property. Fun for all the family. NOT. I bet the only kid who ever liked playing this was Donald Trump. I can imagine the young Donny chuckling to himself as he made his own grandmother bankrupt and homeless.

What's the *second* worst board game in the world?

Pictionary.

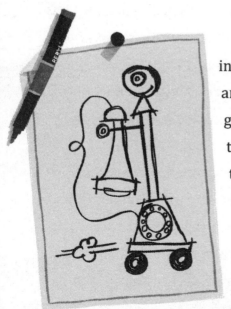

Every Christmas Mum insists we play it. Amber and I are forced to go with a grandparent each, who, once the game starts, reveals that they cannot draw anything from the modern world.

This was my nan's picture of a mobile phone:

And guess what this is?
Alien, anyone?
Grandad's phone rang
as he continued to point
at us and jeer. He paused,
and answered it. 'Hi . . .'
he said, suddenly
going very quiet and
meek – for him.

He listened to the person on the other end,
then spoke.

'Unbelievable! I'll pick the rest up later this week,
you harridan,' he said angrily, and tried to hang up, but
it took him a while to find the right button on his phone.

'Everything OK, Grandad?' I asked.

'Yes! Yes! Fine, just FINE,' he said in a way that
suggested it really wasn't.

'Who was that?' asked my sister.

'Oh . . . just the window salesman,' he explained.

Amber opened her mouth to say something, but
then he started doing his victory lap again.

Later, I looked up 'harridan' in the dictionary, and
apparently it means 'a strict, bossy or belligerent old

woman'. Which I thought was an odd thing to call a window salesman.

The next two days were just so much fun. My new room-mate Grandad Ray and I stayed up late into the night, every night, playing cards. He taught me a game called 'poker', which was much more fun than Monopoly, and he said I was a real natural. He won all my pocket money, but assured me it was a very close game. I also had to write him something he told me was called an 'IOU' (which I now know stands for '*I OWE YOU money*') for the rest of that year's pocket money, after another very close poker game.

I wasn't getting too much sleep, what with the late-night poker club and the bouncy bed from hell. Grandad also snored really loudly, sounding like a zombie with sinus problems.

Getting ready for school was proving problematic too. The entire family had to wait ages to use the bathroom, due to Grandad Ray's intensive showering and grooming routine. All of this was accompanied by him singing at the top of his voice, waking up the whole house at 6am. He had a separate washbag just for his hair products.

Grandad Ray was kind enough to walk me to school, though – but not without asking to borrow my snack money. I gave it to him safe in the knowledge that my VIP fame at the school would mean I could blag some free snacks. Proper famous people never pay for anything. Cars, clothes, watches. Ask yourself this: when was the last time you saw an A-lister wandering around a swimming pool asking for a pound for the locker? Exactly. They get EVERYTHING free.*

Then, a few days into his stay, I got back from school and he was very comfortable with his feet up, reading his newspaper on the sofa. A very loud banging on our front door shattered the silence. I took a quick peek through the front window to see who it was.

'Nan's here,' I cried out excitedly. She was immaculately turned out in a bright pink trouser suit with matching lipstick.

Grandad Ray leaped off the sofa like he'd been electrocuted.

'Don't tell her I'm here, Spike,' he whispered desperately as he ducked down and crawled along the floor into the garden.

What was going on?

---

* Turned out my VIP fame did not extend to free snacks at the school tuck shop. After a scene of public humiliation where, after I'd been asked to pay, I'd told them I was THE Radio Boy and maybe they'd like a shout-out on my show, the blank face of Tuck Shop Theresa meant I had to get Artie to lend me the money.

'Hi, Nan,' I said in a slightly confused voice as I opened the door.

'Hello, darling. Is he staying here, then?' she asked in a very matter-of-fact way. I noticed she had two full black bin bags with her.

'Um . . . no?' I said.

'How do you know who I'm talking about?' she asked.

A pause. 'Well, I assumed you meant Grandad and . . . er . . . he's not here.'

She walked into the house and sniffed. 'I can smell him, Spike, so he must be here. Let me guess – he's hiding and told his own grandson to lie? Typically pathetic.' She wandered off towards the back door that leads to the garden. My sister and I then watched a very sad scene unfold. Our nan searching for her husband and our grandad, who was hiding in our garden.

Just then Dad came home from work.

Amber and I breathlessly got him up to speed with the events of the last two minutes and he joined us at our observation post, the kitchen window.

Our garden is pretty small, so very quickly the Grandad-Ray-hide-and-seek game came to an end. Nan had looked everywhere apart from the shed. My studio.

She rattled the door handle. It didn't turn. It looked like Grandad Ray had locked himself in.

I heard him yell, 'LEAVE ME ALONE, YOU HARRIDAN.'

'That's what he called the window salesman the other day,' I said.

'What?' asked Dad. So I took him through the phone call Grandad had received and the shouting at the window salesman.

'Well, it's finally happened,' sighed Dad. 'She's thrown him out. I wondered what this surprise visit was all about.'

Thrown him out? Can you even throw out a grandad? Aren't there laws against that? The thought of unwanted grandads being thrown out and dumped by the side of the road made me very sad.

So Nan and Grandad argued through the shed door. Nan threw the bin bags on the ground and stormed off. Dad met her as she came back into the house.

'I'm so sorry you all had to see that, darlings,' she said, and Dad gave her a hug. He ushered her into the front room and closed the door.

I went out into the garden to see Grandad Ray. I tried to open the shed door. It was still locked. 'It's just me, Grandad,' I said.

'Is she there with you, Spike? Is it a trap?' he said from inside the shed.

'No no, it's just me, I promise. What's going on, Grandad?' I asked.

'Oh, just your nan having a bit of a meltdown. She'll calm down,' he said. Still from behind the shed door.

'Has she thrown you out, like Dad's just said?' I asked.

'Not exactly, Spike. I'm just being a . . . gentleman and letting her cool off for a few days. She will soon see she's behaved very badly and come back round and apologise.'

I looked down at the bin bags Nan had dumped on the ground.

'Are these all your clothes?' I asked the shed door.

'Yes, erm . . . I . . . I asked her to kindly drop a few extra bits off,' the shed door said.

'Dad, she's gone home,' yelled my dad from the back door. 'So you can stop hiding in the shed now. Come inside when you're ready, we need to talk.' The door unlocked. Inside the shed, the Grandad I saw was not one I recognised. He looked broken.

'Are you OK?' I asked.

'Just thinking about your nan. Hurts like hell, Spike . . .'

Oh no, song time. He grabbed an imaginary microphone with his right hand and pulled it to his mouth:

'Well, since my baby left me . . .'

He sang most of 'Heartbreak Hotel', then sort of slowly stopped and froze on the spot, his mind and heart elsewhere.

He seemed the loneliest man in the world. I didn't want to catch his eye, so glanced around at all my radio equipment crammed into Dad's shed. Grandad must have seen me looking at it.

'This where you do your show, then, is it?' he asked me.

I immediately came alive, telling him how it all worked and where we all sat. Then an idea hit me. 'Hey, Grandad, why don't you come in on the show?' I asked him. 'You could be our first guest.'

Grandad's eyes widened and a smile appeared on his face for the first time since Nan's bin bag dump-and-go visit. It felt good seeing that smile. I was saving my beloved Grandad Ray. No one threw away my Grandad Ray.

GRANDADS ARE FOR LIFE, NOT JUST CHRISTMAS.

'Yes! I thought you'd never ask!' replied Grandad eagerly. He smoothed back his coiffured hair with the silver comb he always carried in his back pocket. 'I guess if you wanted, I could sing . . .' he said, and produced a list of songs he had apparently made on the off-chance I ever invited him on to the show.

'That would be amazing!' I replied. Grandad would be our first live-music guest.

By now, Dad had come out to the shed and must've overheard my offer. I saw him give me a worried look, raise his eyebrows and sigh. I ignored him. 'Come to the shed, our studio, after dinner and we will get you on air,' I said to Grandad.

'Right ho! I'll bring my best stories.'

As it started to get dark outside, I went back down to the shed to get the studio ready for that night's special guest show. I was testing my microphone when Artie and Holly came in.

'Hey, guess what – you know my grandad has come to stay?'

'The one with the big hair, and cowboy boots? Used to sing on cruise ships?' asked Holly.

'Yeah, that's him – Grandad Ray.' I doubt many other grandads fit that profile. 'Anyway, I hope you don't mind, but I've invited him on the show today.'

'Cool, that certainly should be fun,' said Artie, unpacking his vinyl records for the music on the show.

I put us on air and the MIC LIVE sign glowed red, meaning we were broadcasting to the world. But mainly the kids at my school. Midway through our first live link, Grandad came flying in through the shed door, kicking it aside with one of his cowboy boots. It slammed against some paint pots and one fell off the shelf on to the floor.

'HERE I AM!' he shouted. The smell of his aftershave

immediately made us start coughing. He had to duck through the shed door to make room for the hair that followed him. The cowboy boots made him taller, adding to the extra height of the hair. His quiff caught a cobweb, or did the cobweb catch a quiff?

'Erm, this is my Grandad Ray, listeners,' I explained.

'Heyyyyyy, all you dudes out there, how you doing?' Grandad Ray said in a deep fake American voice. Who was he trying to be, a Texan cowboy DJ?

I leaned into the mic. 'He's staying with us at the moment—'

'Yeah, and I'll tell you why I'm currently sleeping in my grandson's bedroom. My wife doesn't understand me and my talents and now she's thrown me out . . . Diane, what have you done?'

Holly watched, her mouth wide open. She needed to be careful she didn't catch one of our resident spiders in it. I don't think she'd ever seen a grandad like mine. But he was only just getting started.

'Only a woman can take your heart and then rip it out, RIP IT RIGHT OUT I tell you, and then stamp on it, STAMP ON IT! . . . And then make you eat it. I hope that evil bug-eyed wit—'

'Grandad, that's my nan!' I interrupted. Sure, he was upset and angry, but no one wants to hear their grandad call their nan an 'evil bug-eyed witch'. I mean, she didn't even own a broom.

Grandad jumped to his feet. His massive hair collected another cobweb. Maybe his hairspray was attracting them like Velcro. He pulled the microphone close to his mouth and started to sing. It was some old song about having a broken heart. His eyes remained closed for the entire song. We watched in shock and awe.

'Whaaaaat becoooooooooommmmeeeeesss of the broken-hearted . . .' crooned Grandad. Everyone was getting the full Grandad Ray experience tonight.

When he finally finished the last verse of his moving performance we all burst into applause, which, in fairness, he had encouraged us to do by means of a cardboard sign he'd made with 'APPLAUSE' written on it in black marker pen.

I played a song.

When the MIC LIVE light went off, Artie spoke first. 'You have a great voice, and what a great song choice, sir. I love Motown.'

'You know Motown music, Arnie?' asked Grandad.

'It's ArT-ie, and yes I love all the old classics,' answered Artie.

'Great to see the younger generation appreciating vinyl – you and me are going to get along like a shed on fire,' said Grandad.

Immediately, he and Artie began an in-depth discussion of the label's greatest hits. United in a love for Artie's old vinyl collection. Bonding over music. I smiled, seeing Grandad so happy again.

Then we were back on air, not that the MIC LIVE flashing light made any difference to Grandad Ray's volume control.

'It's the *Secret Shed Show* and Radio Boy here with the gang and our special guest, my Grandad Ray. Grandad, why don't you tell everyone about what you used to do?'

'Well, I was a professional singer. My stage name was Toni Fandango.'

Holly burst out laughing when she heard the name.

'Something funny, girl?' said Grandad, in a dangerous tone.

Oh no.

'I wouldn't be laughing if I had ginger hair like that,'

Grandad snapped back. Looking around the shed for laughter. He got none.

Uh-oh. One thing you don't ever do is take the mickey out of Holly's ginger hair.

'Well, at least it's not dyed with shoe polish,' Holly fired back.

Grandad Ray looked horrified. Holly glared at him. Sherlock snarled.

'Right, um, shall we move on?' I said. 'So, why the name Toni Fandango?' I asked, in an effort to stop Holly and Grandad's hair wars from escalating any further.

'Well, it was either Toni Fandango or Bobby Gibbon,' said Grandad.

That set Holly off again. I shot her a look.

'I was a proper professional singer,' said Grandad. 'Played on all the biggest stages.'

'Wow! That must've been so exciting, singing to massive crowds in big arenas,' said Artie.

'Yeah, it was. Sometimes it was standing room only in the Kon-Tiki bar on the *Caribbean Queen* cruise. They said when I sang I made grown men cry and women fall in love with me.'

Holly sighed and rolled her eyes.

'What happened?' I asked him.

'Suddenly they didn't want an old-timer like me. Showbiz will eat you, then spit you out. Showbiz is a dog that you think is your best friend, then one day it hits you in the face with a shovel and runs you over in your own car.'

'But dogs can't drive, Grandad,' I pointed out.

'Oh, you know what I mean. Then the only place I could get work was on car ferries. Portsmouth to Cherbourg. No way for a man like me to end up.'

Much to my surprise and Holly's annoyance, the listeners loved Grandad Ray, aka Toni Fandango. The texts and messages poured in, saying how funny he was. It gave me another idea.

'Well, I hope you enjoyed the show and thanks for all your messages. Grandad Ray, you were a great special guest. Who thinks Grandad should join the team every week while he's staying with us?'

'Yeah! Come on, join us,' said Artie, Grandad's new best friend in antique music.

Holly glared at me, but I took no notice.

'Well, thanks, kids, I think I will accept that offer. Always knew I'd be brilliant at radio.'

Ever modest, my Grandad Ray.

And so it was that three suddenly became four. What a nice thing to do for my poor heartbroken grandad.

Also, as I would find out in time, a Really Big Mistake.

CHAPTER 6

Radio Stars Wanted

'Good morning, World!

'Who wants MY JOB?

'Who DOESN'T want my job?

'Chatting to stars.

'Going to all the coolest parties.

'Do you want to be a Radio Star?

'Do you DREAM of being a DJ?

'Becoming a famous celebrity?

'Walking down the red carpet and seeing all the

losers behind the barriers wishing they were YOU?

'*Then keep listening, as we have details on a brand-new talent competition, the first of its kind in THE WORLD:*

'*Radio Star!!!!*'

Wait.

I turned to the radio.

What did he just say?

'*We are looking for a brand-new DJ for Kool FM and it will be one of YOU.*'

Every morning, while getting ready for school, I listen to my most favourite radio show in the world, Kool FM's breakfast show with Howard 'The Howie' Wright.

This morning, The Howie's announcement had just blown my mind.

If you could see my mind before and after this, here's how it would look:

Sherlock stared at me, confused. I guess Sherlock, in his doggy mind, was wondering, '*Why has my master's mind just exploded?*'

It would be like he'd just heard a dog DJ on Paw FM announce that all dogs could now come in and eat for free at the new pizza place in town.

Come to think of it, restaurants are quite boring. I have some ideas on how to improve them:

A Pizza Restaurant for Dogs and Their Owners. I'm serious. Think about it. Who doesn't love pizza? Instead of a plate, they would just bring your dog's pizza out in a large bowl – 12" deep pan, of course. No anchovy and pineapple toppings for our four-legged friends – instead they'd offer toppings like tripe, beef bone, dried pigs' ears and peanut butter. Maybe some dog mouth-mints after that for their breath.

Pizza Mutt, I'd call it.

TV Dinners Restaurant. This is a winner. You all sit in booths with a TV right in front of you. Everyone has their own. You eat your meal in front of the TV. Great, right? No need for boring conversations with Mum or Dad, *'How was school today? What did you learn? Blah, blah.'* We can watch what we want and they can watch some rubbish drama from olden times with posh people in big hats on horses and carts. Everyone is happy.

Anyway.

I had to sit down to take in what The Howie had just said on the radio. My heart was racing. This competition could be my big chance. To break out of my shed and into a real studio. How would Katherine Hamilton feel about the way she'd treated me, then? In a word: badly. I imagined her hanging around outside the Kool FM studio, waiting for me. Then, as I pulled up outside in a chauffeur-driven limousine (or possibly my dad's old estate car), she would throw herself at me, crying as she begged for my forgiveness. Other screaming fans trying to get my autograph. My bodyguard (Sensei Terry) having to clear a path for me. All very realistic, I'm sure you'll agree.

Howard 'The Howie' Wright knew about me and the *Secret Shed Show* – when I'd first started the show, the local newspaper had done a story about it, and he'd given a quote. Surely this would give me an unbeatable advantage in the Radio Star competition?

I couldn't help but think it was mine to win. *Wait till I tell Mum, Dad, Holly and Artie*, I thought. I raced down the stairs two at a time and burst into the kitchen, where I found Mum and Dad by the sink in a very intense conversation – well, shouting and pointing their fingers at each other. All I heard before they quickly spotted me and stopped was:

Dad: 'He will just take over the whole thing and ruin it. We have to get him out of this house, Carol.'

Mum *doing her trademark move (stamping her foot and pointing)*: 'You are being very mean and – Oh, hello, Spike, sweetie, we were just chatting about . . .'

Me: 'Yeah, I know who you were talking about and Mum's right; Dad, you're being really mean about Grandad. But anyway, I haven't got time for this right now. I have far bigger things to think about – stardom, for instance. Listen to *this* . . .'

I turned the kitchen radio on.

'*Good morning! It's Howard "The Howie" Wright here, at ten minutes past eight. We are launching THE WORLD'S biggest-ever radio talent competition, Radio Star!*

'*If you want to be a famous DJ like me, then this is your chance, my friend.*

'*The winner gets personally trained by me, and you will do my very own breakfast show here for a whole week while I'm on holiday in the Caribbean!*

'*It's for anyone and everyone –*

'*Young and old!*

'*All you need to do is send us a short ten-minute tape of you presenting a show. Not a real one if you don't have one, just what yours would sound like if you did.*

'*Good luck! (Terms and conditions apply.)*

'*Let's get the travel news now with Travel Tanya.*'

'Well . . .' said Dad. 'It's really exciting, son, and I'm right behind you as always, you know that . . . but these talent competitions . . . well, they aren't really about the best and most talented winning. Look at *X Factor.*' He patted me on the shoulder. His brown tie was dotted with flecks of toast.

'Your dad's right, Spike, it's probably just a very big marketing idea to get the whole town talking about the station. I heard the other day –' SOUND THE-MUM-WHO-KNOWS-EVERYTHING KLAXON!!! – 'that their latest audience figures are out and they have lost a load of listeners, so that's probably why they are doing this. My friend Denise, who works in the accounts department, told me,' added Mum.

'And a dirt-cheap way to get someone to do his show while he's off sunning himself in Barbados!' said Dad.

'Or . . . they could be looking for the next new super-star DJ!' I said. 'Why are you both being so mean about The Howie? He could be helping me change my life. You heard him, *young and old* – he's talking to me! No one else is a young DJ in this town. He's inviting me to enter so we can work together, master and apprentice. Like Yoda and Luke Skywalker. It starts with looking after his show, sure, but then one day the apprentice becomes the master and I replace him. But that's a few years away. I'm telling you, this is meant to be. I just know it.'

Mum moved over to the kitchen counter and

started doing her daily exercise routine. This involved wearing her gym outfit and bending, twisting and squatting while making mine and Amber's breakfasts. Using bags of sugar as weights and punching the air with them. To any onlooker walking past our house at that very moment and glancing through the kitchen window, it would've looked like a mad woman in leggings squatting down and back up again for no real reason. Like some crazy game of hide-and-seek with strangers, all while waving groceries about.

'One . . . two . . . three . . . OK, Spike, go for it . . . four . . . five . . . six.'

'Just be careful, I don't want to see you hurt – again,' Dad said quietly.

I knew what he was referring to, of course: my disappointment over Fish Face giving Merit Radio to his son, Mutant Martin.

But this competition was not that. It was a *proper* competition run by a proper (and amazing) DJ, where the best person would win. Me.

My phone started buzzing in my pocket and I took it out. Messages from Artie and Holly.

Artie

We're entering, right?

Holly

Kool FM here we come! Hx

The Howie's announcement had reached them too. My uncontrollable excitement was only brought back down to earth at school. The morning passed uneventfully, with lots of 'Did you hear Kool FM this morning? You *have* to enter!'

But then at lunchtime the radio dream bubble burst. Guess who popped it?

'Helllooooooooo, pupils of St Brenda's, this is Merit Radio and your fun-lovin' – that's lovin' with no "g" as you kids like to say – host! Yes, it's Mr Harris here, but you can call me Mr Harris or Headmaster or sir . . .'

'Or His Excellency,' I said loudly. It got a big laugh. I wasn't smiling for long, though.

'*Some* **extremely** *exciting news to share with you all,*' continued Mr Harris. '*Now, some of you may not*

be aware that Kool FM (the FM of course stands for FREQUENCY MODULATION. There's your fun fact for today!) have launched a disc jockey competition and I'm sure you would all like to wish good luck to ...'

Wow. He was going to wish me luck? Fair play. Even with that thick, fishy-scaly skin of his, he knew I was the one to win this. He *had* learned something from what happened between us, after all.

'Good luck to . . . ME! Yes, that's right, I will be entering Radio Star. No doubt you are cheering my decision in the dining hall right now ...'

Cut to silence; total, gobsmacked silence. People looking at each other, frowning and confused. People looking round at me, all thinking the same as me. *Is he seriously entering? Thinking he could do well? Win it, even?* I just shrugged my shoulders and carried on eating my soggy jacket potato. Even the dinner ladies went quiet and laid down their serving spoons to look at each other. And then it got worse.

'Yes, and also good luck to my son, Martin, who will be joining me in our entry, along with the brand-new member of our team ... Katherine Hamilton.'

I dropped the glass of water I was holding. It

smashed on to the dining-room floor.

'Katherine will be doing a fascinating feature called Lost Property Corner. All the latest things left just lying around, so it could be **your** *shoe, gym bag or underpants that Katherine will tell us about, and hopefully we can have some wonderful reunions live on the show.'*

'Reunions live on the show?' Was he mad? Who did he think would hear Katherine Hamilton describe their stinking PE kit and still want to go and claim it live on Merit Radio? Not me, that's for sure. Mainly because my mum had gone to great efforts to sew my name into just about every possible item. In an ideal world, she'd have my name sewn into the back of my neck.

Katherine Hamilton.

Just hearing her name again had caused the blood to rush to my face and I could feel my cheeks turning hot and red. This was the girl I had once dreamed of marrying. Then she went and ruined our future life together by helping Fish Face to find me – by betraying me as Radio Boy. She grassed me up.

Yet even though she threw me to the lions (well, to the fishes), she still had this strange power over me.

And I *had* planned to forgive her one day.

But maybe never now!

Everyone at school knew she was going out with . . . MARTIN HARRIS. My arch-enemy and nemesis. But now she was joining Merit Radio and entering Radio Star, against me! This was open-heart surgery. With no anaesthetic.

Was I in some weird computer game where players had to find new ways of making my life hell? Forget the Sims, this was the Slums.

This was the girl who had called my very own show telling me I was 'the best'. Now she was all aboard the Martin Harris Love Train with his headmaster dad in the driving seat, wearing a train-driver's hat. The three of them against me.

I started to feel sick at the thought of having to hear them together on the radio.

Suddenly all that came into my head was that song Grandad had crooned earlier, which, judging by his voice, sounded like it was called 'What Becomes of the Broken-farted?'.

CHAPTER 7

The warning signs were there from the moment Grandad Ray joined our merry band of radio outlaws.

Dad had warned me too, and I'd ignored him. 'Be careful, son, you are doing a kind thing, but remember: Grandad is very selfish. That's why Nan threw him out.'

I just thought he was being mean – but he was right.

For his second appearance on the show, Grandad Ray carried his own chair into *my* shed studio. The old picnic chair I'd sorted for him obviously wasn't good enough. So he rocked up with Dad's office chair. My dad doesn't actually have an office, it's just a desk and swivel chair in the gap under the stairs. Grandad had hauled the chair all the way into the shed studio, and I soon realised it wasn't for comfort. It was because it was a big chair and higher than any of ours. He now had a sort of royal radio throne, to look down on us from.

It got worse. For the next show I walked into the shed to turn everything on before Artie and Holly arrived, and found Grandad was already in there. Sitting in MY chair, behind MY microphone.

'Just thought we could switch things up a bit tonight,' he said. 'I can do a bit more on air – you know, might freshen things up.'

I stood there, shocked, unable to speak. It was my show. He wasn't just taking *part*, he was taking *over*.

Holly came in and within seconds had assessed the situation and, more importantly, what she could do about it. 'Sorry, Mr Hughes Senior, but that's Spike's chair. I'm going to have to ask you to move, as the microphone is carefully calibrated to his voice and if you speak into it, your voice won't sound as big and strong as it normally does.'

Genius, Holly – appeal to his vanity and ego. She then doubled that up with this:

'Also that's where the spiders' nest is.'

'ARRGGGGHHH!' screamed Grandad Ray as he leaped up and scuttled back to his chair. After the show, I asked Holly how she knew he was scared of spiders.

'You forget, I'm in the Army Cadets. We are trained to notice everything and read people,' Holly said, looking pleased with herself.

'Wow, that's incredible. What a skill,' I said admiringly.

'Yup, that and the fact your mum told me he was,' Holly said.

It had been three shows now and we were heading into tonight's fourth with Grandad Ray on board. It was getting worse. Grandad was holding court midway through tonight's *Secret Shed Show*, telling a long, boring story about performing at some comedy club in Blackpool. Holly was rolling her eyes in boredom and miming yawning behind his back. Clearly, she still hadn't forgiven him for the 'ginger hair' comments.

Artie was politely feigning interest and my face was frozen into a fake grin. I was also trying to swallow a yawn. You know when you desperately need to have a big yawn but you can't when someone is talking to you, as it's too rude? So you have to try to swallow it. Not that it would've mattered if I had let out a huge yawn anyway – Grandad wouldn't have noticed, as he was pretty occupied with what he thought was another fantastic story. The same one he'd told last week, and the week before that, I believe.

'Did I ever tell you about the time the cruise ship I was working on was in a gale force fifty storm?' Grandad asked, when his earlier story had mercifully come to an end.

'Yes, I think you did, Grandad.' But Grandad ploughed on regardless.

'During a song – it was a particularly good rendition of Elvis Presley's "Love Me Tender" – a huge wave, must've been twenty thousand feet high,* at least, rocked the ship so hard I flew off the stage and landed on the front row. I went head first into a lucky lady's bosom!'

'That's enough, Grandad! You told us this story last week and we got a complaint about that last bit from a listener's mum who said it was "inappropriate".'

* You cannot have twenty-thousand-foot-high waves. If you did, the waves would be four miles high. Kinda like Grandad Ray's hair.

'Well, she sounds like a stuck-up, boring old whatnot. I always say if a story is worth telling once, it's worth telling twice,' Grandad said.

'Maybe not for three weeks in a row, though, eh? Let's play a song,' I sighed.

'Song? Do you want me to sing?'

'NO!!!' said all three of us simultaneously.

I hit the play button so hard and quickly the studio desk shook. It was more like a panic button than a play button.

Very quickly my Grandad Ray had overrun the show. Like a rotten apple that stinks out the rest of the thing the apples are contained in. No, that doesn't work. Forget that. He was a *cuckoo*. You know what cuckoos do? A cuckoo lays its eggs in the nest of another bird. Just some stranger bird's nest it doesn't even know. The cuckoo babies hatch out of their eggs quicker than the other bird babies and they just kick them out of the nest, their nest, totally taking over.

Grandad was Cuckoo Ray.

What had I brought upon me, the team and the listeners?

And it wasn't just the tendency to take over. Holly

had started calling him the 'Big Topper' behind his back. Anything you had done, Grandad could top it. Not only had he done it, he'd done it bigger. Better. Scarier.

Like earlier in the show today, when Artie was telling us the story of what had happened to his hair.

'My dad just said my hair needed trimming and he was perfectly able to do it himself. I said, "You're not a professionally trained hairdresser, Dad," but he said he's been making cakes for years using all sorts of hand-held tools, shaping, cutting, trimming – so how hard can it be? Well, when I looked in the mirror I saw how hard it is. Look at the state of me!'

I have to say, Artie's hair was truly in a very bad way. My mum, in her hospital, would have described it as being in 'critical condition'. He looked like he had contracted a rare tropical illness where the poor sufferer lost random chunks of their hair. Although he mostly looked like a kid whose dad had cut his hair.

Guess who'd had a worse cut, though?

The BIG TOPPER, of course.

'That's NOTHING! I was once working in the Caribbean, back in '78, I think, and we stopped off in port. I decided to enjoy some downtime and went to visit the local zoo. Well, it wasn't too long before some of the ship's passengers spotted yours truly and begged me to sing to the tigers; apparently they love a bit of old Frank Sinatra – I mean, who doesn't? So I did. Now this was a pretty shabby-looking zoo that wasn't very well maintained and one of the tigers got out and came after me. I guess it must've really loved my voice. It leaped over the shoddy fence. Who knew the old Toni Fandango magic works on humans *and* animals? Well, I tried running away, but it's not easy in flip-flops, and I tripped, and the tiger was on me!'

'Were you hurt?' asked Artie. He didn't ask out of concern, more in a very bored and tired way.

'I was lucky. The keeper shot it with a tranquilliser dart and it fell asleep on top of me. Stank, it did. But it had taken several chunks out of my hair. So there you have it, I got a haircut from a TIGER!'

The Big Topper had struck again. Artie's dad had butchered his hair. Grandad Ray had a *tiger* ruin his. I couldn't help but feel sorry for the tiger. It would've been coughing up Grandad Ray hairballs for weeks.

The show carried on.

'Call in now,' I said, 'if your older brother or sister has ever done something really evil to you. Yesterday, Amber, my older sister, told me I was adopted and for a few hours I really did believe her. The more I thought about it, the more it made sense. Mum, Dad and Amber all love Marmite; I hate it. The evidence was compelling and overwhelming.'

We got some great calls:

- Dev called in to tell us his older brother once put on a monkey mask and jumped out at him, giving him such a fright he fell down the stairs. Knocking a tooth out.
- Arya's older sister told her that a glass full of vinegar was *delicious* apple juice, so she took a huge swig. And was sick.
- Ryan really wanted to play football with his older brothers. So they let him. Be a goalpost.
- Nadia was invited by her older brother into a 'magic lift'. She spent two hours waiting for it to take her up to Fairyland. To many, this 'magic lift' looked exactly like a bedroom cupboard.

Today was a great show. No way would Merit Radio and the gruesome threesome beat me in the Radio Stars competition.

'I'm a little bit bored tonight, Spike,' said Grandad casually as the record we were playing came to an end. 'Too many flipping kids on the show.' Holly and Artie nearly fell off their chairs.

I managed to say, 'This is the *Secret Shed Show*. I'm Radio Boy. Thanks for all your calls tonight . . .' while inside I seethed.

'Bless them, eh? You can see why there ain't too many radio shows by kids for kids!' said Grandad Ray.

I really couldn't find any words. I stared at the MIC LIVE sign. We were still on air.

'Why do you say that, Ray?' said Artie, in an ominous tone.

'Well, son, I think only grown-ups know how to really tell a story. Even then, it's only a few that are blessed like me to be storytellers. To be honest, kids just aren't very good.'

Artie and Holly glared at him, their eyes burning holes into his head.

It was in that moment that I realised Dad had been

right. Grandad 'Cuckoo' Ray had taken over the show. I glanced at the studio inbox where all our emails and texts came in. It was a non-stop blizzard of listeners asking who this rude old man was, ruining our show. The cuckoo had hatched and taken over the nest. Eaten all the eggs. You get the idea.

'Erm, I don't agree with that, Grandad,' I said. Very quietly. It seemed almost wrong to disagree with him. But scared though I was of upsetting my beloved grandad, I had to defend my listeners. I'd be nothing and no one without them.

'What's that, Spike? Couldn't hear through your mumbling,' he said.

This time I spoke louder and clearly. 'The callers made me laugh, more than your repeated stories. Anyway, that's it for tonight's *Secret Shed Show*. Thanks for listening – maybe next week we will talk about family members who outstay their welcome, or CUCKOOS.'

I killed all the radio mics before Grandad could say anything else to upset everyone. He took off his headphones and smoothed back his hair. Not as easy as it sounds, as the thick hair cream had attracted a few new cobwebs. Grandad quickly brushed them off as if they were a highly dangerous corrosive acid.

'Those kiddies will try even harder next week, Spike, after my pep talk. Tough love it's called, used it on your dad.'

'So kids can't tell stories?' Holly said in a calm but ever so slightly demonic way. She was like a slow-ticking time bomb.

'Look, sweetie, don't get upset. These days all you kids get a pat on the head and told no one is a loser at sports day. Well, it doesn't help you. There are losers in life. Fact.' Grandad Ray replied as he replaced his fire-hazard comb. With all the hair grease on that, if it came within a mile of naked flame we would all go up in a fireball visible from China.

'Like living in your grandson's bedroom at your age? Fact,' Holly replied, winking at him. Psycho-style.

'You don't know what you're talking about, young lady,' Grandad snapped back.

This was going to get ugly. If he wasn't careful, thanks to Holly, Grandad Ray might end up with his trusty comb sticking out of him. Let's not forget she's won karate trophies and is in the Army Cadets. They don't mess about in the church hall where she goes for her cadet training. I'm talking combat-trained kids. She could half kill him within seconds, then field-dress him and save his life. I'd let her, but I'm worried we'd be hearing Grandad's story about it for the next eight years:

'She ripped my head off and shouted down my neckhole, then ripped my heart out and ate it in front of me etc. etc. etc.'

Just then the shed door rattled.

'Dinner's ready!' yelled Mum. Saved by Mum's shepherd's pie. Something I never thought I'd say.

'Great, I'm outta here,' said Grandad as he left the three of us standing in the shed and disappeared back to the house.

The MIC LIVE light went dark.

Everyone started speaking at the same time. Unleashing their fury and anger at Grandad Ray, The Artist Formerly Known as Toni Fandango.

'He's killing our show,' said Artie. He was always the calm one. For him to say such a thing showed how desperate the situation was.

'That was awful, Spike! Did you see the studio

83

inbox?' said Holly, her cheeks flushed with anger.

I could only make out odd words through the wall of Grandad-bashing from them both. But their final line to me was crystal clear.

'You have to fire your grandad.'

CHAPTER 8

In for the kill

'Are you kidding me? Are you actually suggesting I sack my own grandad? A harmless old man down on his luck, whose wife has just thrown him out?'

'YES!' shouted Artie and Holly in perfect unison.

'Yeah, OK, fair enough,' I said. I understood, but the thought of what I had to do made me feel physically sick. You ever had to fire a family member?

'Plus, *harmless*? That man is as harmless as Mr Harris's stinking bad breath,' said Holly. 'He's no cute grandpops, Spike. He's a bitter old cruise-ship entertainer whose career didn't happen.'

Artie was next. 'Your poor dad, growing up with him. I'm surprised he didn't run away and join the circus.'

'I know, I know,' I said. 'But you've seen what he's like. If I sack him, he'll . . . well, I don't know what he'll do. He's pretty . . .'

'Insane?' said Holly.

'Crazy?' said Artie.

'Um. Yes.'

'Well, I'll make it easy for you,' said Holly. 'Either he goes or I go, Spike.'

Wow. Even thinking about trying to do without Holly was crazy. But I *really* didn't want to fire Grandad Ray. I'd won a round of poker one night and he'd thrown the pack of cards out of the window. I dreaded to think what he'd do if I dumped him from the show. I tried to reason with her.

'Yeah, OK, I get it. He's just . . . in a tough spot right now . . . maybe after a little chat he'll be back on form and apologise . . .'

'ME or HIM,' Holly said CLEARLY, SLOWLY and LOUDLY. Then she went in for the kill.

'I'm telling you right now, Spike, you enter Radio Star with *him* on the show, you're guaranteed to lose. Merit Radio will sound brilliant compared to us, with your crazy grandad in our shed. The judges, *if* they are still awake after hearing our entry, with boring stories about cruise ships, will think it's HIS show—'

'OK, OK, I'LL FIRE HIM!' I yelled.

She was right, as always. Radio Star was my big break and I couldn't let anyone get in the way of that. I'd come too far. The thought that they would think it was Grandad's show really got me angry. It was MY show. I was the star. Now I was starting to understand why Dad felt the way he did about him. 'Tough love,' Grandad Ray had said earlier. Maybe he needed a dose of that himself.

By the way, 'Tough Love' sounds like a bad rapper.

'Hi, my name is Tuff Love and I'm here to rock.'

No, you're not. Your real name is Christopher Pringle. You live in your mum's basement and work in a dry cleaner's.

'How do I do it, though?' I asked. 'You've seen him. He's got the emotional sensitivity of a great white shark who hasn't eaten in a month. He'll eat me alive.'

Just thinking about it frightened me. He could be very intimidating with that overly high hair.

'Well, I'm sorry, Spike, he's *your* grandad, *you* invited him to join the show so *you'll* have to fix this,' said Holly.

I looked to Artie for answers. He steepled his fingers and cocked his head to one side, like a wise old owl with some insight to share. I appreciated the fact he was giving my tricky situation the thought it deserved.

'Do you really think a tiger ate his hair?' he said, at last.

CHAPTER 9

The Snake

That night, after we all said our goodbyes, I headed up to bed with a heavy heart. I heard Grandad Ray before I saw him. It was a full-on zombie orchestra in my bedroom tonight, judging from the snoring levels.

Using the kind of subtle, soft footwork a Russian gymnast would be proud of, I tried to avoid stepping on the noisy floorboard in my bedroom and alerting Grandad to my presence. I caught a glimpse of his right arm over the duvet, and the tattoo on it. One I hadn't seen before. It seemed to be of a tiger eating a man's hair. I squinted to get a better look. The man in the tattoo was a barely recognisable version of Grandad Ray. He looked like a large, female Italian opera singer wearing a tiger backpack.

How on earth was I going to tell a desperate and unstable man like him that he was fired from a kids' radio show? I had to sleep on it. On the inflatable bed of nails on the floor, listening to Grandad Ray's snoring as he slept on *my* comfortable bed.

The answer came the next day from an unlikely source.

I leaped out of bed the following morning, before my alarm could wake Grandad. I was also hoping to catch Dad before he headed off to work at the supermarket, but Mum said he'd had to leave early. Maybe no bad thing anyway, as Dad would've been angry with Grandad when he heard how he had ruined our radio show. He might have thrown him out on to the streets! I couldn't ask Mum as she'd just defend him; she was totally under his spell. Or maybe the aftershave fog surrounding him had affected her brain? In her eyes, either way, Grandad could do no wrong.

I headed to school, with my head and heart full of

dread. Sensei Terry was on his post round, with his postbag bursting with letters and parcels. 'Morning, Spike. I see a young man heavy in thought,' he said in his wise karate-warrior way.

'Really? How do you know?' I asked.

'Samurai training. I can read a man easier than a book. If I see someone wiggling their fingers, they could be about to attack with that hand. I've already thought through my options to neutralise the attack. It's over before it's begun,' he said casually.

'Wow! Have you ever had to use this knowledge in practice?'

'Oh yes. A man was once loitering near my car, Spike, looking very shifty indeed. I crept up on him. He spun round and went to withdraw something from his pocket. This could've been a knife or gun so I was compelled to react FAST. The best form of defence is attack. I grabbed him at lightning speed and threw him over my hip, classic hip throw, Spike. Correctly known as O-Goshi. KABLAM! On the pavement.'

'WOW! A knife-wielding maniac?'

'Not exactly, as it turns out. A traffic warden who was trying to get my parking ticket out of his pocket. Still, we had a laugh about it, once he got out of Casualty a few days later. I never did get that ticket . . .'

At that precise moment Grandad Ray came strutting past us. 'Have a good day at school, Spike. This weirdo bothering you?' He gestured at Sensei Terry.

'Oh no. This is Sensei Terry. He's not just a postman, Grandad, he's also the local karate instructor,' I explained.

Sensei Terry, upon hearing his introduction, gave a half-bow to Grandad Ray.

'Karate, eh? Yeah, been in a fair few scraps myself . . .'

Here we go, I thought. The Big Topper at the ready. You might want to pull up a chair, Sensei, we could be here a while as it's Grandad storytime.

'Well, I'm afraid you can't beat the skills learned in the bars and back streets of the Philippines, when eight pirates are trying to attack you. Black belt in karate ain't no good then, other than to hold your pants up, Postman Pat.' Grandad Ray looked at me, chuckling. I didn't laugh back. Nor did Sensei Terry.

'I mean, what would you do if I suddenly went . . . KACHANG!' – and with that Grandad Ray did something incredibly stupid. He tried to grab our postman Sensei

Terry round the neck from behind.

Before I could even get out the words 'NOOOOOOOO, GRANDAD, DON'T', like *you* would do if your own grandad had just poked a grizzly bear for 'a bit of a laugh', Sensei Terry had 'neutralised' Grandad Ray. He effortlessly threw him and his huge hair over his hip and deposited him into the hedge of Number 73 Crow Crescent.

O-Goshi and O-splatti.

'Argghhhhh – my back! I'll sue you for beating up an old man. If I was ten years younger, I'd have smashed your—'

'Grandad, you attacked him without warning.'

'I was just mucking around!'

Sensei Terry apologised profusely and gently helped Grandad up, brushing him down and then pressing his palm firmly into Grandad's back. Something clicked loudly.

'There you go, sir, you should be fine now,' Sensei Terry said. 'Just your third and fourth lower vertebrae were tight.' This man could break people and then mend them again. Awesome.

'Stay away from me, you ninja postman!' muttered Grandad Ray, now back to his normal self. Maybe Sensei Terry could un-mend him, come to think of it.

'Come with me, Spike,' Grandad Ray urged. I stayed put.

'No, I'm OK, actually, Grandad,' I said calmly.

'Suit yourself, then. I've got my eye on you, postie, Sensei Tom or whatever you are,' said Grandad bravely, from well out of Sensei Terry's reach.

We watched Grandad walk away with far less confidence than when he had arrived. He was still muttering to himself as he got his comb out to redo his hair.

'He's the problem on your mind, isn't he, Spike?' said Sensei Terry, watching Grandad walk away.

'Yes.'

'I heard your show. He has . . . taken over a bit,' said Sensei Terry.

I sighed. 'Yes. I need to sort of . . . sack him and I have no idea how,' I replied.

'Ah. You need to take the fox from the henhouse?' asked Sensei Terry.

'What henhouse? It's a shed. No, like I just said, I need to sack him from the *Secret Shed Show*.'

'Exactly, take the snake from the kittens.'

'No, sack Grandad from the radio show.'

'Show the monkey the ape.'

'No, sack Grandad.'

'Remove the frog from the pond?'

'Eh?'

'The cat from the mice.'

'What?'

'Keep the wolf from the door, Spike.'

'What are you going on about?'

'Your problem is one as old as the mountains, Spike. You have to remove the snake.' He pointed at Grandad

Ray, who was now disappearing from our view. Not so much a snake as a slippery eel.

I thought it best that I too spoke in animals with Sensei Terry or this conversation wasn't going to go anywhere.

'Yes! You're right, I do have to remove the *snake*. But I don't want to hurt the *snake's* feelings too much. The old, annoying, singing *snake* has been thrown out by his nice, kind *snake* wife,' I explained. Then I paused. 'Plus, the snake has a nasty bite and might take my head off.'

'This old snake has no feelings, Spike. Tough, leathery skin. You must be quick before he wraps himself further round you.' He paused and rubbed his chin thoughtfully. 'Can I give you some advice, Spike?'

'Not if it involves me throwing him over my hip.'

'No, far better than that. You've heard of the phrase, the pen is mightier than the sword?'

'Are we still talking about the snake?'

'No. The pen is mightier than the sword means that words are far more effective than violence. Words can start or end wars. Words can help you fall in love. What makes you good at radio, Spike? Words.'

'So . . . write him a letter?'

'Yes.'

Great idea, that's what I would do. Write Grandad Ray a letter. Firing him.

Can snakes read?

CHAPTER 10

THE Letter

You know in exams when you have to show all your workings? I'm going to do that here. It's not easy telling your grandad that he is fired from your radio show. I had been taught to respect my elders, but I had to protect the show/henhouse from Grandad Ray/the snake. He was going to ruin my chances of winning Radio Star, and cause Holly to leave.

I knew I had to. He was destroying the show. But I was still worried. Would he get angry with me or, even worse, get upset and cry? Or, much, much worse –

sing? Maybe he would understand and say sorry for being rude to Holly and all of our listeners.

Ha. Fat chance.

Here is the letter with all the attempts to get it right:

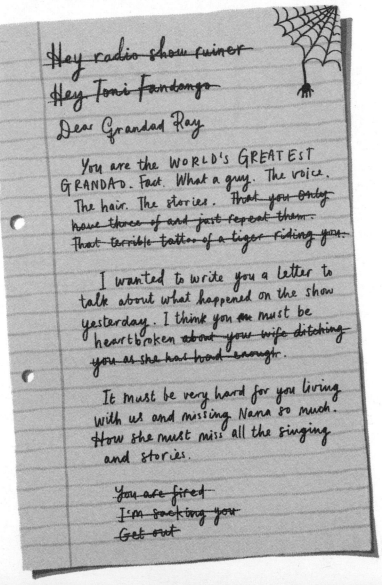

~~Hey radio show ruiner~~

~~Hey Toni Fandango~~

Dear Grandad Ray

You are the WORLD'S GREATEST GRANDAD. Fact. What a guy. The voice. The hair. The stories. ~~That you only have three of and just repeat them.~~ ~~That terrible tattoo of a tiger riding your.~~

I wanted to write you a letter to talk about what happened on the show yesterday. I think you ~~are~~ must be heartbroken ~~about your wife ditching you as she has had enough.~~

It must be very hard for you living with us and missing Nana so much. ~~How~~ she must miss all the singing and stories.

~~You are fired~~

~~I'm sacking you~~

~~Get out~~

This was just so hard.

I stopped and thought about how unkind Grandad had been to Holly. He hasn't been thinking about her feelings, or mine for that matter, when he said my show was basically pants.

I suddenly remembered just how much he loved playing games . . . and winning them. I started to write again.

Let's play a game, Grandad, as I'm having a lot of trouble saying what I mean so maybe this is easiest.

1. What rhymes with 'hack'?

2. What is the opposite of 'you're hired'?

If you guessed 'sack' and 'fired' you are CORRECT. You have got the SACK and are FIRED.

Fun game.

No, seriously, you are fired.

Signed:

Spike AKA RadioBoy

And Holly and Artie and every single person that listens to my show

CHAPTER 11

the RAY-chter scale

The Richter scale was developed in the 1930s to measure the magnitude of earthquakes.

It goes from:

Richter 1.0 – a Microquake which is not really felt by anyone but particularly sensitive ants,

to:

Richter 9.0 – total destruction to all nearby houses, cars, people and animals – any living thing within a 1,000-mile radius of the epicentre.

Well, I can confirm that the Richter people need to

add a whole new level.

Richter 10 – Grandad Ray's explosion upon receiving my letter.

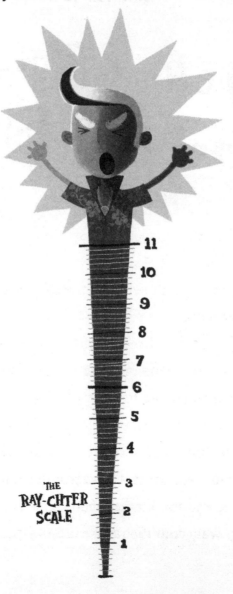

11
10
9
8
7
6
5
4
3
2
1

THE
RAY-CHTER
SCALE

CHAPTER 12

WHEN GRANDads go BAD

We were live on air when it happened. The Grandad Ray earthquake.

It was just the three of us in the shed doing the radio show. Me, Artie and Holly. The way it all started and the way it should be.

At first, we were aware of someone shouting – more like howling, actually. It was similar to the sound you hear from that strange man you often see outside a bus station, yelling at the moon. The howling was coming from outside the shed and, worryingly, it was getting closer. Then the door handle rattled violently! Thank goodness it was locked, as always, to keep my mum out, but I nodded solemnly to Holly to unlock it. I already knew who it was for two reasons:

1. The overwhelming and familiar scent of aftershave, Eau de Pong.
2. Sherlock was growling through gritted teeth by the shed door.

The rotting shed door almost fell off its hinges, as Grandad Ray came flying in. He wasn't dressed quite as smartly as usual. He was wearing only jogging bottoms and a white string vest, revealing his faded tattoos that I could now make out even more clearly, including one I hadn't seen before of a very ill-looking Hawaiian hula girl stretched over his belly.

'Th-th-th-th-thanks for this, GRANDSON,' he spat out as he waved my letter like a fan in front of my now-reddening face.

I didn't need Sensei Terry's psychic powers to know he was a little bit upset.

'We are live right now on the *Secret Shed Show*, let's play a song—' I managed to rush out in 0.000007 seconds.

Grandad Ray shoved Artie's chair aside and grabbed his microphone with his big grandad hands. Why is it grandad hands and ears seem to get bigger as they get older? The secret service should use them as human listening devices to spy on potential suspects.

The MIC LIVE! sign flashed on as Grandad Ray rammed the microphone button down. He had put himself on air to all my listeners. His eyes were wild and I think he was foaming at the mouth.

'Now, listeners, let's have a little CHAT with my grandson. So, Spike, why don't I tell all your Oompa-Loompa-sized listeners, all those sad little Munchkins,[*] about this letter you've written me, SACKING your poor old grandad from this tinpot Kiddie FM show.'

'It's not tinpot,' I protested.

'It is! Boring kids with boring stories. You can't fire me, sonny Jim – I quit!'

'I'm sorry, Grandad, it just wasn't working out and—' Before I could even finish my sentence he cut me off.

---

[*] Munchkins? Oompa-Loompas? For the record, my listeners do not have orange faces, and nor do they have jobs driving candy-cane boats in Willy Wonka's Chocolate Factory.

'I'll show you, and you, and you,' he said as he pointed at each of us in turn. 'You'll pay for this, I promise you.'

Then he stormed out. His comb fell out of his back pocket as he slammed the shed door behind him. It really couldn't take much more rattling and certainly wasn't designed to withstand Earthquake Toni Fandango. We all sat in stunned silence. We felt like earthquake survivors surveying the aftermath damage. Which in this case was the shed door barely hanging on by one hinge.

Suddenly there was more wailing outside the shed studio window. Silhouetted by the moon was Grandad Ray. It was song time again.

'THE WIN-NAH TAKES IT ALL . . .'

'ABBA. What a song,' muttered Artie, with grudging respect.

Grandad had his back to us and his tattooed arms were wide open as he finished his song. From where I was sitting, it looked like he was performing to the moon.

Hell hath no fury like a spurned grandad.

CHAPTER 13

A Spurned Grandad

Every Friday that Grandad Ray had been staying with us, he would have an ice cream ready for me and him to enjoy together the moment I finished school for the week.

It was our thing.

Two days had passed since he burst through the shed door. He'd been very quiet, which was a very good reason to be suspicious. I'd been doing my best to avoid him at all costs. It's not easy in a tiny house like ours . . . and what with the fact we were room-mates.

More like cell-mates. I'm pretty sure he was snoring even louder on purpose.

Each day since he'd started staying with us, Mum had been trying to get him to join a club in the evening. This was something she'd always done with me, too, until I split my pants at Sensei Terry's karate class.

'It'd be good to get out there, Ray, and meet people your own age,' said Mum.

Always trying to fix people. Every day, various leaflets would be thrust in Grandad's face by Mum. Every day this was met with a swift reply.

'I'm not joining a dominoes club with the living dead, Carol.'

'I'm not joining a bingo club, Carol, with losers.'

'I'm not joining a nude life-drawing class, Carol. Not even as the model.'

Then finally, the day after the sacking earthquake, one did take Grandad's eye.

'Ballroom dancing, you say, Carol? Well, well, well. I've always fancied that. I can already move like a pro from my cruise-ship days. I reckon I could have been a world champion disco dancer.' And the Big Topper was off.

When he returned home from his first ballroom lesson, I could hear his booming voice in the lounge boasting to Mum.

'Loads of lovely ladies there, Carol. I've got a date this weekend with one of them. They all loved me when I started to sing.'

Mum's favourite TV show is *Strictly Come Dancing*. Which is, without doubt, in my opinion, the dullest TV show in the whole wide world. Newsreaders and very tanned soap stars in sequins and fake grins looking like wooden puppets.

While I think of it, humans are odd. Why do we dance? I hope at no point in my life am I expected to dance. We must be the only animals that do it. You ever been to the zoo and seen a couple of chimps doing the foxtrot? If they did, of course, it would be awesome. Ballroom Chimps is also a good name for a band. *Strictly Come Chimping*. Now *that's* a TV show I'd watch.

Anyway, as I walked into the kitchen I saw Grandad Ray sitting with an ice cream in front of him. *Oh good*, I thought, *he's calmed down now and is back to his sort-of-loving Grandad ways. Me and him enjoying an ice*

cream. He's finally realised he overreacted. This is his
peace offering. I accept.

He saw me walk in, and, without looking up, started
to carefully unwrap the ice cream from its silver foil
packet. Slowly and methodically, he proceeded to eat
it. Where was *my* ice cream? Was it waiting for me in
the freezer? No, it wasn't. There clearly wasn't an ice
cream for me.

I never knew it was possible to eat a choc ice in a
threatening and menacing manner – but Grandad Ray
managed it.

As he was committing this act of family war,
I spotted something red and angry on his forearm. It
was a fresh tattoo.

'Seen it?' Grandad growled at me.

I had. In blood red, the word 'FAMILY' was freshly
etched into his skin. He turned and stared into my eyes.

Sherlock must have sensed something was up as
he suddenly leaped across the kitchen and jumped
at Grandad Ray, knocking his hand and the ice cream
straight into his face.

Grandad Ray spluttered, snorting ice cream from
his nose.

'Ha ha! Good boy, Sherlock,' was all I could get out through my hysterics as I ran from the kitchen followed by a tail-wagging Sherlock. *Serves Grandad right*, I thought.

'Funny, is it? Manky old dog with a ridiculous name!' shouted Grandad Ray angrily after us.

I ran into Dad. He always showed up when there was trouble.

'How are things between you and Grandad, since you asked him to leave the show due to . . . um . . . artistic differences?'

'Pretty odd, Dad, actually. He's changed into some kind of monster.'

'*Changed*, Spike? He's always been like that. I told you. Look, I may have my differences with him but he loves you. Just give him some time – his very large ego has taken a bit of a knock over the last few weeks, with your nan kicking him out and now you sacking him . . .'

'He was ruining the show, though!' I protested.

'I know, I heard. You did the right thing. You could have come to me and I'd have dealt with it, though.'

'I didn't want to hear you say "I told you so",' I said.

'Which I said just now, didn't I?' Dad asked.

'Yes.'

'OK, sorry. He will be OK soon enough. He's landed on his feet in this new ballroom-dancing club by the sound of it. He won't want to be staying here for much longer.'

How wrong he proved to be.

CHAPTER 14

Please, Dad, NO

As if Grandad going to the dark side wasn't bad enough, my house was about to be rocked (literally) by a brand-new revelation. Not from Grandad this time. Not from Mum. Or even from my sister, Amber.

This was, in fact, from the most sane person in my family, which after me was my dad.

That is what made it even more shocking.

'You're reuniting your band?!' said my stunned mum dramatically.

'What's the big deal, Carol?' said a poor man caught

in the headlights of an oncoming Mum-shaped ten-tonne truck.

'YOU ARE A GROWN MAN! WHAT WILL PEOPLE SAY?'

Bingo! Classic Mum catchphrase. 'What will people say?'

To be honest, I had to agree with my mum. This was a shocker. Dad used to be in a band, The Pirates, and by all accounts (mainly my dad's) they were pretty good. Good enough to get a record label interested in signing them. Sadly, though, the lead singer, Tom, had got 'involved' with my dad's sister, Aunty Charlotte, and had not behaved, according to Mum, 'like a gentleman'. Midway through their song 'Dance Like You've Got Scurvy', Dad punched Tom live on stage. A full-on Pirate bundle commenced! Unsurprisingly, this band of merry Pirates was never quite the same after that on-stage fight, and nor was Tom's voice. Dad's punch knocked a tooth out, causing him to lisp a little when he sang.

However, it would appear that after twenty years of not talking to each other, Facebook had brought the Pirate mateys together again and the band had had a reunion in the Bunch of Grapes pub last week. Dad had apparently 'forgotten' to tell Mum he was going. She only found out the next morning that he hadn't gone out with some of his supermarket colleagues, when she'd received some 'intel' from her network of spies. Other mums: always on the lookout for each other.

My sister and I were united in something for once. Embarrassment. Amber spoke for both of us when she said:

'Er, you won't be playing in public, will you?'

'Well, actually, yes,' Dad said hesitantly. 'We are going to use Tom's garage this weekend to rehearse, check the magic is still there, and then the plan is . . . next week . . . we take part in the monthly Battle of the Bands at the Red Lion.'

THE RED LION!

The Red Lion was a pub mainly frequented by people with huge amounts of hair but very few teeth. My supermarket-manager dad was thinking about playing in a band there with a load of old people who hadn't played together for decades. *Does he have a death wish?* I wondered.

But Mum was already ahead of our concerns.

'The Red Lion? You'll be killed. It's a pub for serial killers and hobos.'

'No, it's not. They got rid of hobo Carl last month. You are scaring the kids, Carol.'

My parents only used each other's names in serious arguments.

'Well, YOU are embarrassing them. Men your age should know better.'

'Thanks for the support, Carol. It's just a bit of fun.'

At that moment Grandad Ray wandered in. Combing his quiff. The aftershave pong was at an all-time high. People in China were probably sniffing the air wondering what that horrific smell was.

'Can't talk for long, hot date with Theresa from my ballroom club.'

Lucky Theresa. Hope she has a gas mask handy.

'Now, what's this about a reunion for the Pirates? Is it due to *no* public demand? That band were bad years ago, let alone now,' continued Grandad Ray, smirking.

Dad shot straight back: 'Well at least we *got* record label attention, Dad, which I don't think you ever—'

'I WAS BORN AT THE WRONG TIME,' Grandad retorted, so quickly his quiff shook. It always moves as one. Like it's a living, breathing organism. It could have its own nature documentary. 'When I was in my singing prime, record companies moved away from proper music, to that rap rubbish with kids miming and pretending to sing songs. Just nonsense. Can you auto-tune HEART or SOUL? I don't *think* so. That's why you and Artie play real music, Spike . . .' he said, and looked over to me for support. *You're not getting any*, I thought, as my mind flashed back to him eating that ice cream. *You're on your own, Grandad.*

He glared at me. Rubbed his newly inked 'Family' tattoo. Yeah, I see it, Grandad – how about you practise it and GET MY ICE CREAM!

'Kids, can you just give us a moment, please?' said Dad as he ushered us out. GET IN! The timeless 'Kids, can you give us a moment, please?' is in my Top Three Mum and Dad Classics.

My Top Three Mum and Dad Classics:

1. 'Can you give us a moment, please?' Always mid-argument. Translated, this means 'THINGS ARE ABOUT TO GET REALLY UGLY' and the

very moment you are thrown out of the room you IMMEDIATELY begin listening in – usually with a glass pressed against the wall or simply by sitting in utter silence, holding your breath.

2. 'I'm going to count to three/four/five/ten and then . . .' A staple Mum or Dad fall-back. The nuclear countdown sequence. You only ever start to do anything once the countdown has been activated.

3. 'Don't make me come up there.' This, I reckon, has been said since people lived in caves. Hard for it to be taken seriously back then though, as stairs hadn't been invented. I guess cavekids just stood looking confused. Of course it would've sounded like 'Ugg un ug ug bah eck eck eck ohh ohh ug ug' – which, roughly translated, means, 'If I find out you've been scribbling on the cave walls again, it's straight to bed for you with no raw mammoth.'

Amber and I left as instructed, while Dad gently guided us out like a dad bouncer or security guard. We took up our positions on the stairs, after audibly thudding up them, then gently, like ninjas, creeping halfway back down again. Crouched. Spying.

We heard it all. Dad was talking angrily.

'You never ever supported my dreams, Dad. It was always about you. No wonder Mum has had enough—'

'It was just tough love, son. I couldn't lie to you, your band sucked.'

It was hard to understand what happened next. We heard what sounded like a table being moved out of the way really quickly, Mum yelling 'No, don't hurt him,' and then Grandad Ray running out of the kitchen at over 100mph.

CHAPTER 15

BREAKing DAD

Bad news.

Dad's band rehearsal went well. This may sound mean, but just think how you would feel if it was *your own* dad. Think of him right now. Go on – your dad. The slippers. The terrible dress sense. The unfunny jokes. Now imagine him playing the drums in a band he was in decades ago. On a stage. Where people can see him. Dressed as a PIRATE! Someone there tells someone who tells someone and then word gets around the school. You see my situation now. Horrific. That 17 per cent cooler I told you about earlier, thanks to being

Radio Boy? Well, back to zero for me.

I'm starting to realise my life is like a game of snakes and ladders. Any moment when you think you are winning, back down you go. A scandal like this could ruin my school life forever. Doesn't matter if you invent a cure for the common cold in your biology class and change life for millions of people, if you have an embarrassing parent you'll only be known for that. Like poor Miles Baker. Miles is the best choir singer in the school and has won loads of awards. Doesn't matter. There is a rumour that his dad has three nipples. He's Miles Baker and is famous not for his beautiful voice, but his three-nippled dad.

Look, my dad's band have a song called 'Pirate Party in My Pants'.

This is the level of embarrassment we are dealing with.

So, following their successful rehearsal, tonight at the Red Lion my dad and his old band The Pirates were going to enter the monthly Battle of the Bands.

After school, me, Artie and Holly cycled past the pub. It looked rough. Broken windows, and hairy bikers hung around outside menacingly, smoking beside their huge polished chrome motorbikes. Some of them looked over at the three of us and I'm pretty sure one licked his lips like we were a snack.

'Please don't kill my dad tonight,' I whispered as we speedily pedalled off.

'OK, status update: I'm now officially scared for my dad's safety,' I told Artie when we got back to the house.

'Dads are invincible. Mine told me so. They have

superpowers,' said Artie.

'What do you mean?' I asked.

'Well, for example, how else can dads tell if you really are sick or just pretending?' said Artie.

'You're right. They just *know* if you're lying and chucking a sickie. Dad Jedi mind trick.'

'And who else knows which people to trust?' Artie continued. 'My dad says I should never trust a man with a beard. I said what about Father Christmas? Dad said even *he's* shifty. What else is he doing the rest of the year? Does he pay the Elves the minimum wage?'

This made sense. My dad was always warning my sister Amber about various men not to trust, for future reference.

THE TEN COMMANDMENTS OF PEOPLE
YOU MUST NEVER TRUST
according to my dad:

1. Thou shalt not trust any boy who wears low-slung denim jeans that hang round his backside.
2. Thou shalt not trust anyone who has eyes too close together. Or no eyes.

3. Thou shalt not trust anyone who eats coriander.
4. Thou shalt not give the time of day to anyone who owns and uses a selfie stick.
5. Thou shalt never trust anyone who wears crocs.
6. Thou shalt not trust anyone who has more than three cats.
7. Thou shalt not trust anyone who has more than two cats.
8. Thou shalt never trust anyone who owns a car with a sign saying 'Princess on board'.
9. Thou shalt not trust anyone who doesn't like pizza.
10. Thou shalt not trust anyone who doesn't enjoy watching *The World's Strongest Man*.

My dad's favourite TV show is *The World's Strongest Man*. I love watching it with him every Christmas, with my mum providing a running commentary on the medical damage these various man-mountains are doing to themselves.

'*That blond Viking-looking man from Iceland could burst a blood vessel straining like that! He looks like a sausage on a barbecue that's about to burst. Why is he*

trying to pull a huge truck? If it's broken down, you just call roadside recovery.'

My dad was most certainly not the World's Strongest Man. He often had trouble opening jars. How could he protect himself if the bikers and hobos at the Red Lion didn't accept the invite to 'Pirate Party in their Pants'?

Then it hit me. I knew someone who could protect him. The *only* person who could protect him. Sensei Terry.

When Artie had gone, I quickly cycled to Number 19 Crow Crescent and pulled up at Sensei Terry's house. Outside his front door were two samurai garden gnomes locked in a bitter battle for front-garden supremacy.

I pressed his doorbell. Ancient chimes rang out followed by a loud gong. The door opened and what greeted me was a vision I will remember for years to come. It was our local postman, the one-man neighbourhood watch and karate instructor, dressed in a red silk Japanese dressing gown. 'Kimono' I was later informed is the correct term. He was holding a mug that said 'World's #1 Postman' on it but he had scribbled out 'Postman' and written 'Karate Master'.

His kimono was a thing of shimmering beauty. It also looked very flimsy and highly flammable. I think this was 'Japanese' by way of 'Dodgy Dave', the man who sells knock-off clothing at the market. Fake brands that are just spelled slightly differently. Giorgio Armandi, Hugo Moss, Kelvin Klein.

'Spike, everything OK?' he said, looking concerned.

'My dad's about to be attacked by serial-killer hairy bikers,' I blurted out.

'Now?' hissed Sensei Terry. His muscles tensed as he said the word. Always ready for action.

'No, later tonight after he's had a party in his pants.'

'You'd better tell me what's happening,' Sensei Terry said, and invited me in.

I got him up to speed. The Pirates. The reunion. The rehearsal. The gig tonight. The Red Lion. The Battle of the Bands. The old men. The party in the pants. The imminent danger of death by angry bikers.

'I can help,' said Sensei Terry quietly.

'How?' I asked.

'I can go to the pub and be the band's head of security.'

'But I don't want Dad knowing – he'll get angry with me,' I reasoned.

Sensei Terry frowned, thinking about all this for a moment.

'I will be undercover,' he replied.

'Under . . . cover?'

'As a hairy biker,' said Sensei Terry. 'Now I must go and ready myself.'

With that, he wandered off. I imagined some ancient meditation ritual he would undergo. Cleansing mind and body; preparing for the battle. Of the bands.

As I got back on my bike to head off home, I looked back through his kitchen window, hoping to catch a glimpse of these sacred rituals. Instead, I saw Sensei Terry with his hand in the biscuit tin. I guess those ancient samurais frequently readied themselves for battle with a few Chocolate Hobnobs beforehand.

CHAPTER 16

The Rumble at the Red Lion

I'll never really know what actually happened that night at the Red Lion. All I can be sure of is that no one could have predicted it.

Let's look at what I *do* know about that fateful night.

I waited up until Dad got back. Partly to see how he got on, and also to check he had survived the hairy bikers and serial killers.

And, lo and behold, he opened the door and came in, singing to himself, at just past midnight.

We can tick one box:

✓ Alive

I'm guessing it must've gone quite well as he came back a little – how shall we say – 'tired and confused', and his singing sounded very jolly. I think beer may have been involved. He went into the living room where Mum was watching TV and I couldn't hear what they said to each other, but when they came out into the hall I heard Mum say, 'I'm so proud of you, Mr Puppykins' and then I felt a little bit sick. I guess this is what happens when you eavesdrop. 'Mr Puppykins'? Urgh. Let's move on quickly.

Anyway, that's another box ticked:

✓ It obviously went well.

The next morning, while I was dishing out a tin of stinky tripe chunks to a grateful Sherlock, I quizzed Dad about how it went. Do *you* find that getting information out of your dad is sometimes like interrogating a spy, caught behind enemy lines? He gives very little away. Even if my dad became world champion at chess and solved global warming in the same day, all he would say when I asked how his day was, would be, 'not bad'. If Mum had done all that, she'd be wearing a T-shirt saying it and a plane would've written it in the sky.

Dad says it's like being at a press conference, being questioned by us.

So, this is our post-Battle of the Bands press conference, conducted over breakfast.

Dad is on one side of the kitchen table. On the opposite side are Amber and me. He doesn't have a microphone in front of him, just a cup of tea and toast.

Me: 'Dad! How did it go?'

Dad: 'Yeah, good, Spike. Amber – at the back, by the cereal – do you have a question?'

Amber: 'Hi, yes. How was it? I mean, playing with your old band twenty years later, what was it like?'

Dad (picking his nose): 'Good fun.' (mumbling)

Me: 'That's it? "Good fun"? Nothing else? How were the crowd?'

Dad: 'OK.'

Me: 'Just OK?'

Dad (reading his paper): 'Yeah, all good.'

Enter Mum, who chucks in a GRENADE!

'Did your dad tell you they WON the Battle of the Bands?!'

Me, Amber, Sherlock: 'WHAT!!!!!!!!!!!!!!!!!!!!!!!!!!!!!!!??????'

Dad: 'Yeah, we won.'[*]

Dad and The Pirates beat six other younger bands. Incredible. The fearsome Red Lion crowd got very unruly, apparently, demanding that the band do an encore!

I was looking at my very own dad, while taking in this information, and seeing him in a totally different light. It was hard, as he was dressed in his light brown supermarket-manager suit and tie. How odd for him to go from crowd adoration last night, to checking the stock levels of satsumas and Coco Pops the next day.

I could imagine him at his tiny desk in the store room, daydreaming, reliving that gig. Dad at the back behind his drum kit, furiously driving the band's formidable sound. Looking at Dave the guitarist, now an insurance salesman, then at Tom the lead singer, now a successful owner of several tanning salons, and smiling at each other. All feeling it. My dad lost in a trance, hearing the band's name announced as winners. Then rudely snapped out of his happy memories with a 'Sorry, Mr Hughes, we have a spillage on aisle nine'. Livin' the dream, Dad, livin' the dream.

---

* I used tiny font to indicate barely audible mumbling.

My sister, Mum and I all patted him on the back as he headed out the door. Before he left, he turned to me, leaned in and said, 'I *think* I saw Sensei Terry there last night.'

'Really?' I said.

'Well, it looked like him, but for some reason he was wearing a long-haired wig and dirty biker jacket,' Dad said.

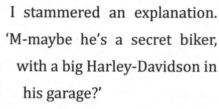

I stammered an explanation. 'M-maybe he's a secret biker, with a big Harley-Davidson in his garage?'

'I saw him leave on his postman bike, though.'

'Yeah, er . . . strange . . .' Now it was my turn to mumble and give nothing away.

After he closed the door Mum said, 'Well, I think that was a lovely adventure for your dad that ended well.' She crossed her arms. As if saying, 'All's well again in the Hughes house.

Harmony has been restored in the family galaxy.'

But neither Mum nor me had any idea that Dad's band adventure was far, far, *far* from over.

CHAPTER 17

Please, ~~Dad~~, No (part 2)

BREAKING NEWS!! Something extraordinary has happened. Something . . . terrible. Something I don't even think I can put into words right now, because it's so unbelievable.

I'm still trying to process it all. There just aren't words to describe the events that followed Dad winning the Battle of the Bands last night. To explain, I'll just give you a timeline of the last two hours and eighteen minutes. As a military report:

15:47

I come home from school. Boring day. Double maths. Physics. Games. Hell.

16:07

Older sister Amber comes home from school. Shuts herself in her bedroom and talks non-stop on the phone to someone who may, or may not, be a boy. At least it's not a pony. My sister's pony, Mr Toffee, is a money pit. I wanted a new pair of trainers, but was told we couldn't afford them until next month because Mr Toffee had a vet's bill. The bill was for a DENTIST! A pony dentist. This pony has better dental care than I do. How do you even get a pony into a dentist's chair?

16:47

Mum gets a phone call downstairs. Normally I'd pay no attention, but what makes me stop and take notice is the fact that she starts speaking in an unusually high-pitched voice and is struggling to find words. Stuttering, awkward silences, then 'Yes, sorry, I'm still here, it's just such a big thing.' It's clearly a very 'big thing' as then several phone calls are made by Mum, excitedly relaying it all back to the League of Extraordinary Mums. Let me introduce them.

A powerful trinity. Make no mistake.

17:33

Dad comes home. Enters kitchen. Mum asks Amber and me, 'Can we just have a moment, please?'

We retreat to our observation post on the stairs.

Sign language is required to bring Amber up to speed on what I've overheard. We shrug our shoulders to each other a few times, indicating we have no idea what on earth is going on. The possibilities are:

- Mum is having another baby. This is good news on one major count: there won't be enough room for Grandad, so it'd be BYE-BYE, Grandad.
- Grandad Ray has been arrested for crimes against hair-manity. Again, great news.
- Dad is seeing one of the dinner ladies. What will people say? (I can't believe I'm thinking that. Help! I'm turning into my mum.)

17:35

We can hear Mum and Dad speaking in deliberately quiet voices, but the content is clearly too explosive for them to sustain that safe volume level and very quickly they are shouting. Then the door is opened suddenly.

'Very funny, Spike,' says Dad. 'Nice one, good prank call for the *Secret Shed Show*. Well, you got your mum good and proper. She fell for it, look at her face.'

Mum is confused. I am too.

(((137)))

'Sorry, Dad, I have no idea what you are talking about.'

'Yeah right, you think I'm going to fall for that? That someone from *Search For a Star* was at the Red Lion show last night? Pull the other one, son – you're not kidding *me*.'

'DAD, I DIDN'T CALL YOU!'

I have my serious face on. I am desperately trying to convince Dad of my innocence. Wait, did he say *'Search For a Star'*?

'You didn't?'

'What did they want?' Amber asks.

Dad is still in silence, frowning, trying to work it all out.

'A producer from *Search For a Star*, looking for new acts, saw the Pirates and invited them on to the live auditions . . .' Mum trails off, barely believing herself what she is saying.

'Hang on, a live audition, as in ON THE TV?' I spell it out just in case there has been some misunderstanding.

'Yes, son,' says Dad quietly, still frowning. 'I guess I better call them back.'

So there you have it. The big news.

MY DAD'S GOING TO BE ON *SEARCH FOR A STAR*.

That's correct. You didn't read that wrong . . . This country's BIGGEST TV show that gives false hope to wannabe members of the public who think they can sing/dance/entertain. And Dad's band are going to be on the live auditions. Which everyone from my school will see. Live. On their TVs.

17:47

Grandad Ray comes home.

'What's happened here? Looks like you've all had some bad news.'

'Dad's going to be on *Search For a Star* with his band, Grandad!' I burst out excitedly.

'Yeah, nice try, but you can't kid a kidder, Spike,' he says, and wanders past us.

'No, Grandad, he really is – they won the Battle of the Bands last night at the Red Lion. A producer was there from *Search For a Star*. They want them on the live show.'

Grandad Ray looks like a man who has just received the very worst news he could. Yet in the kitchen his son is screaming excitedly after his call to the producers of the TV show and is sharing the news with the band.

'They'll just be on the show as one of those oddball novelty acts that people laugh at,' Grandad Ray says to us, but more to himself, I think. The snake is jealous.

18:01

Is he the novelty act? I hadn't even thought about that. I just guessed it was because they smashed Battle of the Bands. I now feel sorry for Dad, protective of him. I've seen how cruel the audiences are on those shows, never mind the judges.

As my mind races, it then occurs to me that if people are laughing at him, they will also laugh at me. My life will go back to being even worse at school. All cool points for being Radio Boy and doing the *Secret Shed Show* will be gone. He will be *my* three-nippled dad.

PLEASE, DAD, NO! For your sake and mine.

18:03

Text from Artie:

Artie

Is ur dad going to be famous? You must be so proud. Big up Mr Hughes!

18:03

Text from Holly:

Holly

Are your dad and his band going
to be on SFAS? OMG! This is
AMAZING NEWS! Also, great for
for the Secret Shed Show.

18:05

Feed Sherlock.

As I do, I see Dad in the kitchen by himself.
Drumming, using French loaves as drumsticks.

CHAPTER 18

Grandad Ray Rattles cages

When I came downstairs the next morning, Grandad was in the kitchen holding a broomstick and dancing with it.

'And a one . . . two . . . cha-cha-cha . . . and a one . . . two . . . cha-cha-cha. Just working on my cha-cha for ballroom,' he said, looking up at me.

Whatever. At least the lucky broom had no sense of smell. I think he'd just poured a bucket of Eau de Pong on himself.

'Um, right,' I said.

'Oh, and you won't be the only one in this house doing a radio show,' he added.

I stared at him. I was aware he was trying to 'rattle my cage', as I think it's said. My Grandad Ray was a ten times World Champion Rattler of Cages. Undefeated.

'What?' He'd rattled my cage. TO THE MAX.

'Yep, me and a few ladies from my ballroom class. Daphne, Jackie and Susan,' he said proudly. 'And another thing. We're going to enter that Radio Star competition. May the best man win, Spike.'

'Doing *what*? None of you know the first thing about broadcasting or how to do a show!' I said angrily. The hinges were off my rattled cage doors!

'Well, I saw what you and your muppet mates do. Didn't look that hard. I'll be telling a few stories and singing, the girls and I will talk about ballroom and the olden times when things were better. Better music, better movies, better TV, all better years ago . . . even better kids,' he said pointedly, looking at me when he said the last.

'I have Holly as my producer who knows how all the equipment works, but you . . . you can't even work the TV remote!' I countered.

143

'Well, actually, I have my own Holly. I've got Susan. She runs the electrical shop in town. Could teach Holly a thing or two,' he said. If Holly was here right now and heard that, she'd use that broom as a lethal weapon on Grandad.

'You have no studio!' I pointed out.

'Yep, I do. My bedroom.'

'That's MY bedroom!' I fired back. My voice going all high-pitched, I was so upset.

Oh boy, he was really something. Not only was he deliberately trying to get his own back on me for firing him by ruining my dreams and entering Radio Star – he was also doing his radio show from MY BEDROOM. 'Oh yeah, well who's the one in the bed? ME. He who has the bed rules the room,' he replied.

'Can't see anyone wanting to listen to people just moaning about the good old days. Mr Taggart, my AV teacher, told me that radio is—'

Grandad, as always, cut me off before I could finish my point.

'A zee teacher?'

'A . . . V . . . Audio Visual. Sound and vision. Anyway, he said radio is about making people feel good. Not bringing them down.'

'I know how to make people feel good. Been doing that all my life since the day I was born, with my gift to the world. My voice,' said Grandad.

Well, that made no sense. How could Grandad have been singing as a baby? Though I don't doubt he was born with that big-haired quiff of his.

'You wanna know what one of the best love songs ever is?' Grandad Ray continued.

'Not really,' I sighed. I was finding this all very exhausting and upsetting. At the back of my mind I was thinking how all reality shows and competitions love 'crazy' old people like him. And what's better than one crazy old person? *Four* of them. It was like AGEING AVENGERS ASSEMBLE on the radio.

I'd disregarded his threat to make me pay. Now it was all starting to get a bit too real. He seriously wanted to beat me and win Radio Star. Maybe even more now that his own son was going to be on the TV.

'Well, it's great to have a little competition, isn't it?' I said, trying to convince myself.

'Great – ask me *when* I'm doing my show,' he smirked again. Rattling the cage time.

'When, Grandad?' I sighed wearily.

'Wednesday nights,' he announced.

'THAT'S THE SAME TIME AS MINE!'

'Nice to have a little competition, like you said, Spike. You OK? Don't look too well? And a one . . . two . . . cha-cha-cha.' And off he went, back to dancing with the broom.

This was terrible. Reality shows and talent competitions really do love old folk, almost as much as they love cute kids. As I walked past the hallway mirror, I caught my own reflection. It's just a shame I'm not cute.

CHAPTER 19

EVERYONE'S a DJ

'*Good morning, everyone! Howard "The Hooooooowie" Wright here on Kool FM!*'

Howie was always very enthusiastic about his own name, I noticed.

Note to self – I need an abbreviated radio name that rolls off the tongue.

Spike 'The Hughie' Hughes?

Spike 'The Hugh-Man' Hughes?

Spike 'Hugh Know It Makes Sense' Hughes?

'*Ten minutes past eight on the big one, KOOL FM.*

So, folks, next Monday we start taking your entries for
RADIO STAR . . .'

Howard Wright played the theme tune to Radio Star,
which featured some high-pitched singers all going

'Radio Staaaaaaaaarrrr

You wanna go faaaaarrrr

You can with Radio Staaaaarrrrrr.'

Then a big American-style voice-over yelled:

'ONLY ON KOOL FM AND HOWARD "THE HOOO-OOOOOOOOWIE" WRIGHT IN THE MORNING.'

YES, THAT'S RIGHT, EVERYONE, I'M LOOKING FOR A NEW DJ FOR KOOL FM AND IT COULD BE YOU! I WILL PERSONALLY TRAIN YOU AND THEN YOU WILL LOOK AFTER MY SHOW FOR A WEEK! ALLOWING ME TO ENJOY A LOVELY WEEK OFF AT MY VILLA, GOLDEN SUNSET, IN BARBADOS. NOW WHAT'S STOPPING YOU? THIS IS OPEN TO ANYONE, WHETHER YOU'VE DONE ANY RADIO BEFORE OR NONE AT ALL. JUST SEND US THE BEST TEN MINUTES OF YOU TALKING OR DOING A SHOW AND I WILL SELECT MY NEW PROTÉGÉ — MY RADIO APPRENTICE EXTRAORDINAIRE! YOU COULD BE THE NEXT STAR IN RADIO. AND REMEMBER, FOLKS: ENTRIES OPEN NEXT MONDAY, AND YOU HAVE UNTIL THE FOLLOWING FRIDAY TO GET THEM IN. THAT'S RIGHT: FRIDAY NEXT WEEK IS THE FINAL DEADLINE FOR RADIO STAR! GOOD LUCK AND MAY THE BEST DJ WIN!

My stomach felt like a colony of butterflies had taken up residence. It was fluttering non-stop with excitement and a little fear. This time next year, if I won Radio Star, I could be rich enough to move into a mansion. Or at least get those trainers I wanted.

This was it. Destiny was calling me. *Trained by Howard 'The Howie' Wright.* Who else would be better in this town than me? No one. *'Do my show for a week.'* I dared not even imagine it. I might faint.

I could just see it now. Me, Artie and Holly in that super high-tech Kool FM studio. I bet it was huge. No cobwebs or spiders in that one, and I bet Howard had a special chair like you'd have on a spaceship – not like the pink fold-up picnic chair I had.

My phone buzzed with excited messages from Artie and Holly.

Artie

> Did u hear hat oh Coward Wright's show?

His texts sometimes have typos as he never checks them before sending.

Next Monday entries open Spike. Clock is ticking. I'll make a plan of action.

Her Tuesday-night Army Cadet training at the community centre meant that this would now be run like a military campaign, certain to involve a detailed list being made. Holly *lives* to make lists. She probably has a list of her favourite lists. Holly is the most efficient and organised person I know. Not only is she the smartest and toughest in the Army Cadets, she is also feared in Sensei Terry's karate club. She is a lethal weapon, though you would never know it if you met her. Like a red-haired, pixie-faced ninja.

I was excited, just like Holly and Artie, but that lovely feeling evaporated quicker than a sugary doughnut in Artie's mouth, when I thought of Grandad Ray. How could he possibly launch his own radio show and try to steal Radio Star from me, the rightful winner? Surely he wouldn't really do that? Maybe he was just saying all this to wind me up, get his own back. Or so I tried to kid myself. I knew my grandad well enough to know that he could easily start a radio show just to prove a point. I also knew something else for a fact. He would do everything in his power to try to win. Stopping at nothing.

I was out of our front gate and heading to school when I saw Sensei Terry with our post.

'Ah, Spike,' he said, 'I need some advice.'

'After looking after my dad, and protecting me from Fish Face, I am forever in your debt. How can I help?' I asked.

'It's about karate and you,' he replied.

'Oh no. I'm not coming back to your club after the last time,' I said fearfully. Just the memory of my mum making me go to his karate class wearing my sister's karate pants and them splitting was enough to bring me out in a cold sweat.

'No, no, not that – but when the time is right, maybe you will come back one day and begin your journey in the martial arts. The force is stronger in you than you think,' he said.

'Maybe, but my journey ended in my pants splitting. How can I help?'

'Radio karate,' he said, somewhat eagerly.

'What?' I said.

'I'd like to start my own karate show,' he said, looking at me for approval.

'You?' I blurted out in a slightly ruder tone than I meant. It was an unexpected and surprising development that my local postman and one-time karate instructor now also wanted to do his own radio show. I can't say karate and radio seemed in any way connected. Much like you wouldn't associate cats with unicycles.

He frowned at me.

'Sorry, I meant – wow, Sensei Terry. Who exactly would this show be aimed at?' I asked in the politest way I could. Surely I didn't need to spell out to him that his target audience might be just a bit small?

'Well, I imagined there must be lots of like-minded fans of the martial arts. Also I thought I could include some neighbourhood watch information.'

Sounded like Vigilante FM.

'OK, sounds great, but how can I help?' I said.

'Well, I think I need a list of equipment and advice on how to – you know – *do* it,' Sensei Terry replied.

I wanted to give him no help whatsoever. I wanted to tell him that radio is a highly skilled art like his precious karate and not everyone can just 'give it a go'. I can't roundhouse-kick and he can't just decide to start his own radio show. But I never said any of that.

'Sure, I'll come round with Holly and she can give you the list of what you need and explain how it works.'

With all that confirmed, Sensei Terry bowed respectfully. Something made me glance back at my house. I saw Grandad Ray spying on us and he quickly hid back behind the curtains. I bet his mind was spinning, trying to work out what was going on. Thing is, I wish *I* knew. Why was everyone around me trying to do my thing?

CHAPTER 20

CATastrophe

You never want to see your best friend crying. It stops you dead in your tracks.

Artie burst into tears the moment he got to school. When I say 'burst' I really do mean *burst* into tears. Imagine a massive water balloon exploding.

At first I thought he must've forgotten his cakes for lunch. But no, this was serious.

His beloved cat was missing.

I have a dog, Artie has a cat. Or had a cat. This says a lot about us. Artie just *would* have a cat. Like him, his cat is nervous, skittish and constantly hungry. You never see a cat turn down food. No cat in the history of cats has ever said to its owner when offered food, 'Do you know what? I'm good, thanks.' Same with Artie. OK, cats prefer birds, frogs and toads to chocolate brownies (Artie's favourite) but still there is a similarity. I've often looked at Artie's cat and thought, *If I fell asleep right here and now on Artie's sofa, this thing would try to eat me.* No conscience. No loyalty. Just looking out for themselves and their cat tummies.

I didn't want to say it to Artie, but that cat would probably eat him too, given the chance. Just munch him up if Artie nodded off and the cat hadn't been fed an entire Sunday roast in the last nine minutes.

My other well-researched observation about cats is that they are always disappearing for hours and sometimes days. Where do they go? What do they get up to? Do they meet up with other cats and laugh about their silly owners who give them dumb names like Mr Poppy Kins and speak to them as if they were human babies?

'Oh, hello, Mr Poppy Kins-si-winsey. Oh, he's wanting a cuddle today, well Mr P. can have a ickle

wickle cuddle. Oh, how playful Mr Poppy Kins is today, no, don't scratch me, that hurts Mummy . . . ARRRGHH MY EYES.'

That's the other thing with cats. They turn into furry psychos and attack you for no reason. Some of you reading this may own a cat. Good for you. Just remember: DO NOT FALL ASLEEP IN FRONT OF THEM. Or if you do, keep one eye open.

Also, you are not your cat's 'mum' or 'dad'. If you were, that would be:

a. Really freaky

b. Really amazing.

Did I tell you Artie's cat was called Mr Bun Face? Yep, it was very hard not to laugh a little as your best friend was wailing on his knees in front of the entire school about the disappearance of Mr Bun Face.

'Oh, where are you, Mr Bun Face? Are you dead? Flattened on the road? Will I ever see your cute little face again OH WAH-WAH-WAH.'

As we tried to help Artie off his knees and out of the puddle of tears, Holly and I were assisted by Mr Taggart, who had come to find out what the wailing noise was. We tried to lift Artie to a nearby chair in the school's front office. This chair was dangerously close to Mr Harris's office. I could almost smell his honking fish breath from there. It took some effort, and our first attempt ended with the four of us – Artie, me, Holly and Mr Taggart – doing some weird ballroom waltz back out of the school doors as if we were bouncers throwing out a drunken customer.

Eventually we moved him into the chair.

Mr Taggart, our AV Club teacher (Audio Visual, Grandad) and the man who had secretly risked his livelihood by helping us set up the *Secret Shed Show*, spoke gently to Artie.

'Is your grandad ill, Artie? Your dad said at parents' evening he'd had a nasty fall. It can be very sad to see our beloved grandpas and nanas getting older and frailer as time passes by—'

Before Mr Taggart could go any further, Artie, through streaming eyes and a very snotty nose, managed to blurt out the words, 'Bun Face'.

Mr Taggart frowned in utter confusion. 'Has he hit his head? Is he concussed? Asking for buns! Poor lad,' he said, looking at Artie in a very concerned way.

Holly and I glanced at each other, trying to work out

who was going to tell him. Holly nodded at me.

'It's his cat, Mr Taggart. It's about Mr Bun Face,' I said.

'Bum face?' asked Mr Taggart in a startled way and quite loudly. So loudly it got someone's attention.

'Who is yelling rude words in the halls of MY school?' bellowed Fish Face, our beloved headmaster, as he came barrelling out of his office.

'Apologies, Mr Harris, this poor boy is very upset and I'm just trying to get to the bottom of it,' explained Mr Taggart.

Mr Harris just stared at me. His eyes burning into mine.

'Well, well, well. If it isn't my three favourite pupils. What's up with the king of cakes and turntables?' asked Fish Face in his usual menacing manner. Holly stared back at him, unblinking, while I broke out in an immediate cold sweat.

'His cat, Mr Bun Face, is missing. Artie loves his cat,' Holly explained.

There was silence from all of us now.

'Is the thing dead?' spat out Fish Face, who really needed to work on his bedside manner.

Artie started wailing again.

'No – it's – missing,' said Holly, through gritted teeth.

Mr Harris was clearly not a cat owner. I guess he kept pet sharks. His next words were just about the worst thing you could say to a concerned cat owner.

'Well, it will either be dead on the road somewhere, killed instantly if it's lucky, obliterated, or you will never see it again, as it will most likely have just run away like those feline creatures tend to do.'

Wowzer. Heart of gold, that man. Subtle as a brick. Funnily enough, Mr Harris's words hadn't comforted Artie in any way. In fact, they had the opposite effect.

Artie suddenly looked very pale and threw up on to the shiny polished school floor. The headmaster had overloaded Artie's emotionally sensitive circuits and his breakfast was now on display all over the place. Joyously, some of the breakfast surprise had made its way on to Mr Harris's shoes. Brilliant. My day was already made. Nice one, Artie. Awesome!

'Oh my goodness! Disgusting!' screamed Fish Face as he yanked his handkerchief from his top pocket and covered his own mouth, looking away from Artie's breakfast, which was coating his previously shiny floor and his equally previously shiny shoes.

'Get the caretaker and take this boy to the nurse,' instructed Fish Face behind his hanky-covered mouth as he ducked back into his office/lair, slamming the door behind him so hard it shook. Later on that day there were stills bits of dried Coco Pops on his shoes, which delighted any pupils who were lucky enough to see them. What a surprise that would be later when Fish Face got home from work and went to take his shoes off before feeding his pet sharks.

Mr Taggart, Holly and I guided Artie to the school nurse, Miss Clench, and as we walked Mr Taggart whispered to me.

'You know what to do for Artie, don't you, Spike?'

'Get him some deodorant?' I replied.

'No – but, er, yes, you should do that as he does smell a bit now – but I meant you need to help him find Mr Cake Face.'

'Me? How can I help find his cat?' I asked.

'Use the *Secret Shed Show*, Spike.'

'Huh?'

'You have an audience. You can get people searching for this cat of his,' he urged.

'Really?' I asked. But I was starting to see the logic of it.

'You have to be aware, Spike, that ideas and material are all around you. The best radio DJs and comedians talk about real life. This would make a great competition entry – I mean, what great radio, the search for your sidekick's missing cat.' With that, my audio and visual mentor Mr Taggart gave a wise nod. The buddha of broadcasting.

Yes! Genius, Mr T.

That night I would call upon our listeners to help find Artie's cat. They love a mission. We would do a good deed. *And* help my Radio Star entry.

CHAPTER 21

Cliffhanger

The music coming from my bedroom wasn't the first thing that got my attention. It was the sound of a woman giggling. No, *two* women giggling. I nervously pushed the door open a few inches to see what was going on.

Grandad Ray was dancing with a woman I'd never seen before. Two other ladies I'd also never seen before were watching and clapping in time to what I think was some sort of ballroom dance music. I only knew this as it sounded like the stuff on Mum's fave TV show, *Strictly Come Dancing*.

Grandad Ray had the lady in a very tight embrace and was twirling her around with a ridiculously pompous look on his face.

I need to remind you that this was not the Grand Ballroom of Blackpool Pier. This was my very cramped bedroom, so the other two ladies had to sit awkwardly on my bed (or should I say Grandad's bed), while Grandad and his dance partner waltzed around a space no bigger than a broom cupboard.

'Spike, I can see you there lurking by the door – come on in.'

Oh no. Caught.

'This, ladies, is my grandson Spike who I was telling you all about.'

The three ladies all cooed and made 'Isn't he cute?' noises.

'Spike, meet Susan, Daphne and, last but by no means least, Jackie . . .'

Jackie was the lady he had been dancing with. She curtsied in front of me.

'Just doing a quick foxtrot before we broadcast our first *Ballroom Banter* radio show,' said Grandad Ray, grinning slyly and waving his hand to the corner of his temporary home in my bedroom.

'Erm, where's my bed?' I asked. Noticing the lack of my inflatable bed from hell.

'I had to move it out so we can do the show,' explained Grandad.

A couple of microphones were positioned on stands

on our fold-out picnic table (I had the chair in my shed studio). It was a basic set-up like ours in the shed, but still very capable of going live to the world. Well, to anyone who wanted to hear an old man tell the same three stories over and over again, while some ladies talked over each other. *Nothing to worry about here*, I thought.

'Well, have fun, everyone, and good luck,' I said.

'Oh, I *will* have fun, Spike,' said Grandad smugly.

This whole situation was insane. I was about to go into our garden shed and do my radio show, while my own grandad was about to start his radio show, deliberately at the same time, in MY OWN BEDROOM.

I walked past Dad as I headed out into the garden towards the shed studio.

'Spike, don't worry,' Dad said. 'He will be bored in a week's time. What you do is brilliant and takes proper hard work. That's something Grandad is allergic to.'

'Yeah, thanks, Dad. I gotta go get ready,' I said. I couldn't help but notice as I walked away that Dad had a new haircut. But it wasn't his usual boring 'dad haircut'. It was a new style that clearly required hair gel. Was TV changing him already? These talent shows change people and not always for the best. I hoped Dad was going to be OK. Would he start wearing earrings or make-up next? That would make it even worse when he was on TV. I'd never be able to go to school again.

Sherlock trotted eagerly alongside me as we made our way to the shed to set up for tonight's show. I was, as always, excited when I opened the creaky old shed door and entered my hideaway.

Tonight I had a plan. I wanted to help my friend Artie find his cat, Mr Bun Face.

Holly arrived first. All business, calm as ever, and focused. 'You heard from him?' she said, referring to the man in question, Artie.

'Nah – I'm sure he'll be here soon, though. I've never seen him so upset,' I said.

'Artie is a big softie. You know he plays the cat music?'

'What?'

'Yeah, he told me not to tell you in case you took the mickey,' said Holly, smiling. 'I've been *desperate* to tell you for ages,' she said.

'Does Mr Bun Face tap his paw to the music or do air guitar?'

Holly and I both started laughing.

'What's so funny?' asked Artie as he opened the shed studio door. We quickly stopped laughing. In the way that people do when it's obvious they've been laughing about something to do with you.

'Just . . . my . . .'

Think, Spike, think.

Holly was looking at me, also saying, with her eyes, 'Think, Spike, think.'

'My silly old Grandad Ray. Starting his *Ballroom Banter* show tonight; what's he like, eh?' I said. Relieved I had thought of something.

'I'm not stupid, and, Holly – you are many things, but you're a rubbish actor. Spike, when you lie you get high-pitched.'

'No, I don't,' I said in a very high-pitched voice.

'See!' said Artie.

Holly came clean. 'Look, we were worried about you and wondering if you'd come tonight. Spike said he'd never seen you so upset so I said how much I know that cat means to you—'

'Mr Bun Face, Holly – not "that cat". Who are you, Fish Face?'

'Sorry, I meant Bun Face, *Mr* Bun Face and . . . I . . . told Spike that you play him music.'

'YOU TOLD HIM? I TOLD YOU NOT TO!' yelled Artie. His arms flailed wildly in the air, knocking an old tin of paint off the shelf and on to the floor, narrowly missing Sherlock by a few precious inches.

'Spike, I know you will never let me forget this and laugh about it from now until eternity,' wailed Artie.

'Well, that's a bit dramatic,' I said. I helped Artie sit on his chair. 'You know how much I love my dog Sherlock. I talk to him all the time,' I said, hoping to make Artie feel better.

'Do you?' asked Artie.

'All the time. You love your cat and you love music. I get it. It's really sweet,' I said.

I looked at Artie, who seemed utterly broken, and I remembered my plan.

'I want to try and help find your cat, Artie. The best way I can do that is with the show. So tonight we launch the hunt for Mr Bun Face.'

'What?' asked Artie quietly.

'I know you'd help me look for Sherlock,' I replied.

'I don't know what to say . . . um, thanks,' mumbled Artie.

'It's the least we can do and it'll be fun. Everyone listening will want to help, Artie. I'm sure of it. Our listeners love being set a new mission and this is it. What should be our first song on the show tonight, Artie?'

Artie rummaged around in the bottomless bag where he kept his vinyl records and then looked in the storage boxes in the shed.

'Got it,' he said.

Time to start the show. I pushed the fader buttons up that turn our microphones on, and the bright red MIC LIVE sign glowed.

'Hey, everyone, what's up?' I said. 'I'm Radio Boy, and welcome to the *Secret Shed Show*. With me as always are Artie and Holly, and tonight's show is all about looking out for your friends. Two-legged and four-legged. Let's play our first song tonight. Artie is missing a friend of his and he needs your help in trying to find him. I'll tell you more after this . . .'

I played the song. Blink-182 and 'I Miss You'. Good call, Artie, as ever.

What a cliffhanger.

Who wouldn't be staying with us to hear what happens next? I thought to myself.

This was the kind of advanced radio skill Grandad Ray and his gaggle of ladies could only dream about.

CHAPTER 22

 CAT-NAPPED

The song ended.

'Radio Boy and the *Secret Shed Show* here. Now, listen up. Artie's cat has gone missing and we need your help. Give us the facts, Artie, please,' I said.

'Yes, thanks, Radio Boy. I feel silly getting so upset but he's my cat and, you know, if you have a pet, they're your special friend. They get excited when they see you after school. They follow you around. He's never gone missing before,' said Artie.

'So what's his name?' I said for the benefit of the

listeners and just because, frankly, the name of Artie's cat was worth a show on its own.

'Mr Bun Face,' said Artie, in a matter-of-fact kind of way. Like it wasn't at all odd that a cat had the name Mr Bun Face.

'Mr Bun Face . . . I guess because his face looks like an iced currant bun or perhaps a Chelsea bun?' I enquired.

'No, my cat looks nothing like a cake! That would be weird. No, I just like the name,' said Artie as if that made the slightest bit of sense.

He clearly had cakes on the brain and didn't even know it.

'Where were we . . . yes . . . Mr Bun Face. You liked the name, of course. So, what do you shout if you want to call him? What name does he answer to, just in case one of the listeners spots him? Bun Face or Mr Bun Face?' I asked sensibly.

'MISTER Bun Face, of course, duh,' said Artie, as if I was being a bit slow.

'Anyway, we need to find Mr Bun Face. Artie, can you describe him?'

'He is a very tubby cat, and he needs to go on a diet.

He is black with four white paws, that make him look like he is wearing socks.'

'So why didn't you call him White Socks?' I asked, in all innocence.

'Enough with the names!' shouted Artie.

'Sorry! Where are you, Mr Bun Face? Can we all have a lookout for him, please.'

I played another song.

'I'm getting sightings,' said an excited Holly as if she was reporting from the front line of a military operation. She was right: there'd been quite a few texts and emails.

'You have a caller ready, Spike. He's called Ted.'

'Great, thanks. On line one?' I asked.

'We only have one line,' she said.

'I know, I just like to say it,' I said. I flicked on the phone line. 'Radio Boy here on the *Secret Shed Show*, thanks for the great response in trying to find Artie's cat. We have a caller on line one. Ted, hello?'

'Hi, Radio Boy, I live a few doors down from Artie – you must know me, Artie, it's Ted? Ted Perkins?'

'Nope, never heard of you,' said Artie.

'We used to play together at nursery. You ate all my

lunch once,' caller Ted said, to all our amusement. Well, mostly all. Artie looked aghast.

'I-I-I-I don't remember that. Anyway, Ted, have you seen my cat?' stammered out Artie.

'Yeah, old Mrs Birchem was feeding him last night,' Ted said.

'What! That crazy old lady? My dad said he went and asked her if she'd seen Mr Bun Face and she said she hadn't. When did you say you saw him there?' asked Artie.

'Last night,' said caller Ted.

'How do you know?'

'I was using my new Super Interstellar 5000

telescope and having a nose around. The planets can get a bit boring after a while. I actually saw you dancing in your bedroom in your underpants last week, Artie,' said caller Ted, again making me and Holly laugh, but not Artie.

'Lies, all lies!' said Artie, shaking his head and crossing his arms defiantly.

'But,' I pointed out, 'if Ted saw Mr Bun Face with this Mrs Birchem last night and then Mrs Birchem told your dad she hadn't seen your cat . . . that means someone is telling lies.'

'Well, sounds like Ted is full of them tonight,' said Artie, still smarting from the scoffed-lunch and bedroom-dancing bombshells.

Time for another song. Another downer. Some old band called REM and a very long and sad, sad song called 'Everybody Hurts'.

'Holly, I'm thinking we need to check out caller Ted's report,' I said while the very sad-sounding man wailed the long sad song out around the shed.

'You thinking what I'm thinking, Spike?' asked Holly.

'I hope so,' I said. 'Do you have your Army Cadet binoculars with you?'

'Of course, in my backpack here. Never know when they might be needed,' she said.

'Can I borrow them a second?' I asked.

'Sure,' she said as she handed them to me. I tested the binos out by focusing in on Grandad Ray's room. I could even make out Grandad Ray's gold sovereign rings on his fingers as he stood up, unmistakably clutching a microphone and singing. Those poor listeners to the *Ballroom Banter* show. Did he actually *have* any listeners?

'These are amazing, Holly. Fancy doing some spying? Go and take a look at this Mrs Birchem's house with your binos?' I asked.

'It's called *reconnaissance*, not spying, and refers to the *covert* – that means secret – gathering of *intel* – that's intelligence, or information to you. And the answer is yes,' said Holly, who was sounding like she had swallowed the Army Cadets manual, which I couldn't rule out.

'Great, take your phone so we can get your "intel" live on air,' I said.

'On it!' said Holly as she slipped out of the door. Leaving Artie and me in her wake, both in silent awe.

It would take her only a few minutes to get from Crow Crescent on our less posh housing estate to Artie's mansion and Mrs Birchem's evil cat lair across the road.

Meanwhile, back in the shed, the miserable song about sadness and hurting was thankfully coming to its dreary end.

'Well, this is live radio, Holly is on her way to Artie's to have a look at Mrs Birchem's place after a tip-off from caller Ted who said he saw Mr Bun Face round there being fed . . . Wait . . . I can see Holly is calling in, so let's go live to the scene right now . . .'

I put Holly live on air.

'You there, Holly?' I asked eagerly.

'In position. I can see Artie's house – well, mansion—'

'Gateaux Chateau is not a mansion!' cried Artie.

'It is! You could fit mine and Holly's house, plus all our listeners' houses, inside your lounge, no problem,' I said. 'It's so big it has three postcodes!'

'Can you two be quiet and focus!' said Holly. 'I need calm. I'm scanning the south-facing rear of Mrs Birchem's property. Nothing illegal, I'm merely observing,' said Holly.

'What can you see?' asked Artie. Keen for some good news.

'Wait! She's opening the back door! She's calling out and banging a plate,' Holly whispered excitedly.

I was on the edge of my seat.

Judging from texts coming into the show, so were our listeners. This was radio gold. It was *definitely* going in our ten-minute compilation for the Radio Star competition.

'Let me get closer so I can hear what she's saying,' Holly said, and we heard rustling as she obviously crept closer to get a better position. Then . . . 'I don't believe it!' said a surprised Holly.

'What?' said Artie angrily.

'It's Mr Bun Face all right, I can see the one, two, three . . . four white paws, but she's calling him a different name!'

Artie looked like he was going to throw up. For the second time today. Just *not* over the equipment, Artie, please – maybe over those miserable songs you've got in your bag instead.

'What's the new name?' I asked.

'Mr Pickles.'

'It's MR BUN FACE,' yelled Artie as he banged his clenched fists on the table.

'It gets worse. The cat formerly known as Bun Face has been lured in by her. I repeat, Mr Bun Face has been picked up by Mrs Birchem and taken inside! You know what this is?' asked Holly.

'No,' we both said at the same time. On tenterhooks.

'A cat-napping.'

CHAPTER 23

Face to face with a CAT-NAPPER

'I'm calling my dad right now,' Artie yelled as he leaped to his feet in anger. Rightly so. I'd ended the show on a cliffhanger so I could wait for Holly to return, and I was struggling to calm him.

Finally, Holly arrived back at the shed, breathless from running. 'You can't call your parents, Artie,' she said, already guessing what he would want to do.

'Why on earth not? That grumpy mad old woman has stolen my cat,' said Artie. It was hard to argue with him.

'Then they will go round to the house, she will deny she has him like she did last night and they say what? *"Well, Mrs Birchem, actually we were spying on you, first with an intergalactic telescope and then with Army-issue binoculars, and we know Mr Bun Face is inside"*? She'd just shut the door and call the police.'

'Well, what do we do, then?' Artie demanded. Silence descended on the shed. Broken by the very loud music coming from within my house. It sounded as if an entire salsa band was in my bedroom. It was Grandad Ray, of course. The band may have been in that huge quiff of his.

'It's just Grandad Ray . . . carry on,' I said.

'This is a time for cool heads and calm thinking,' said Holly. 'I know what we do; gather round.'

So we did, as Holly drew a map of Mrs Birchem's house, Artie's house and the nearby park. A very detailed map.

She took us through the plan.

'I'm not doing *that* bit,' said Artie.

'You don't need to, I will,' said Holly. 'We do this tomorrow at sixteen-hundred hours.'

'Huh?'

'Military time – 4pm to you civilians,' she said jokingly. I *think* she was joking.

We went our separate ways, as per Holly's plan, Artie and Holly back home and me back into the madhouse. Grandad Ray was holding court in the kitchen to a fed-up-looking Mum and Dad.

'Well, the ladies said I was a *natural* at radio. I couldn't argue – at least *someone* in the family is, eh?' said Grandad Ray as he laughed into my face, nudging me in the ribs at the same time.

'I'm heading up to bed, big day tomorrow,' I said.

'Good show?' asked Dad.

'Yeah, full on,' I replied, cagily. I didn't want to get high-pitched now and give the game away.

After kissing Mum and Dad goodnight, I sped upstairs and into Grandad Ray's room/my bedroom, and took out the recording device I'd hidden in there earlier to capture his first show. I quickly hid the recorder until I had more time to listen back to how the world's worst DJ and grandad had got on.

NEWSFLASH

9 DAYS

216 HOURS

12,960 MINUTES

777,600 SECONDS

UNTIL ENTRIES CLOSE FOR RADIO STAR

CHAPTER 24

Spooking the ENEMY

School carried on unremarkably the next day. The school had let Artie put up some 'missing' posters for his cat. Whenever I see those missing cat and dog posters on lamp posts, I always think they should consider putting some lower down, at cat and dog height. Just so they can see them too. A dog might recognise the photo and think, 'Oh, I saw that guy down the park earlier'. Also, the posters stay up for ages and ages. We never get to hear whether they are actually found. Are they still missing? Might be nice to put a new one up saying: 'FOUND! TURNS OUT MR CUDDLES WAS ASLEEP IN THE SHED. HA! CATS, EH?'

Anyway. The three of us met up straight after school by the top gate. Ready to free Mr Bun Face from his old-lady cat-prison. Holly went over the plan.

'I'm still not doing *that* bit,' said Artie.

'We know!' said Holly and I.

We headed off towards Artie's house, then I went one way and Artie and Holly the other. The plan was that I would knock on Mrs Birchem's front door and ask her about Mr Bun Face, saying how I was helping Artie look for his cat and generally keep her talking. Holly would make her way from the park at the back of Mrs Birchem's house, to her back door. She would then open the back door (hopefully it would be unlocked) as a cat escape route and place a walkie-talkie just outside. Artie would lovingly call for Mr Bun Face into *his* walkie-talkie and, once he was safely out of the house, they would grab him and run for home!

At home would be his favourite meal ready in his bowl for him. Canned tuna. Yuck.

As I approached Mrs Birchem's house, my walkie-talkie

buzzed with 'Eagle One and Two in the nest'. That was Holly's code for when they were in position. She was Eagle One, Artie Eagle Two. I was Eagle nothing. Great.

I buzzed back: 'Eagle *nothing* heading to the bad place.' 'Bad place' was code for Mrs Birchem's.

I made my way down the overgrown path and knocked on the door. After a short while the door opened and what greeted me was the face of a terrifying cat-napper. I had never seen such evil before in my young life. The old woman was wearing huge thick glasses, so big they made her eyes appear twice the size of her head. She had a small puckered mouth and was holding a knitting needle in her hand.

I smiled meekly while in my head I thought, *Please don't kill me with a knitting needle and then cut up my body and feed it to Mr Bun Face or Mr Pickles as you now know him, you crazy cat-napper.*

'Oh, hi, Mrs Birchem. I hope you can spare me a moment. It's very sad,' I said and pretended to start crying.

'What is up?' snapped a very raspy-sounding Mrs Birchem, who had the kind of croaky voice you hear in TV adverts with old people warning you not to smoke like them.

As I repeated the script agreed with Holly, round at the back of the house the rescue mission kicked in. Artie and Holly told me what happened later.

Artie's version: Holly pushed through a thick hedge and into Mrs Birchem's garden. She ran in some odd bent-over fashion to the back door.

Holly's version: At approximately sixteen hundred hours I made my way through the perimeter hedge that separated the park and the suspect's property. Adopting a low crouch position to blend in with the natural terrain, I approached the south-facing back door.

Artie's version: Holly opened the back door and did something inside, came back out smiling, then put the walkie-talkie by the door.

Holly's version: I checked the back door and fortunately it was unlocked, so I made my way into the kitchen and placed a single iced bun on the table. A sign to the suspect we had been there, but nothing she could really prove. A sign and a warning. Leave Mr Bun Face alone or we'll be back.

Artie's version: I yelled, 'MR BUN FACE . . . HERE MISTER MISTER BUNNY FACE' into my walkie-talkie. My heart burst when he came running out. Running because he loved me, and missed his daddy so much.

Holly's version: The cat came running out because Artie had a plate with three entire cans of tuna on it. I picked up the walkie-talkie, closed the back door and retreated to the RV.

RV is apparently code for 'rendezvous point' – or meeting place, to us 'civilians'.

In other words, my shed. Artie took Mr Bun Face home and Holly came back to the shed to brief me on what had happened.

'You never said anything about leaving the bun!' I said.

'It's an old army tactic. Mind games. Spooks the enemy. During the night soldiers would sneak behind enemy lines and leave a message like 'We were here' and do nothing else. The enemy would wake up and get freaked out,' she explained. I made a mental note to never, ever make an enemy of Holly.

'Well, the cat's back so that's all good. Mission accomplished. Great teamwork. And thanks to caller Ted.' I was overjoyed. The *Secret Shed Show* had come to the rescue.

Then my phone rang and I saw it was Artie. Must be

calling to thank his good buddy for doing this.

'Great to be reunited with Bun Face?' I said.

'We got the wrong cat!' said a shocked Artie.

'WHAT!' I yelled.

'Mr Bun Face has just walked back in. This other cat, the one we took, has three white paws and a *bandage* over his other paw! We have stolen that poor woman's cat.'

And left her a bun, I thought.

CHAPTER 25

Returning to the scene of the crime

'We have to put it back,' I said.

'Well, obviously!' said Artie. 'But how? Luckily my parents aren't back yet from the bakery so they haven't seen that we are now the proud owners of *two* cats. What on earth are we going to do?'

I could hear munching noises in the background at his end. He would be eating his way through some cakes, I imagined, with the stress of all this. Either that or it was the new cat enjoying its tuna.

'I'll ask Holly,' I said. We chatted and another plan

was hatched. This one involved putting the stolen – or as I preferred to put it, 'borrowed' – cat back.

I took Artie through it and told him to try not to worry, we were on our way over. It wasn't too late and not dark yet, so I told Mum we were doing some revision round at Artie's. Holly and I arrived quickly at Gateaux Chateau – Artie's mansion – and were greeted by a sweating, shaking mess of a person. Holly tried to calm Artie down by grabbing both of his shoulders, staring deep into his eyes and saying calmly, 'It's g-o-i-n-g to be OK.'

We found Artie's cat-carrier/portable cat prison and gently got the stolen – no, *borrowed* – cat into it. He looked like he was doing time in there. All that was missing were some tattoos and an orange jumpsuit.

We placed Artie's dad's huge skiing jacket over the cat prison and I carried it, hidden by the jacket, over to Mrs Birchem's house. I made my way down the overgrown path once more, this time with her cat hidden under a jacket. Nothing crazy about any of this. I remembered how I'd promised Mum and Dad I'd stay out of trouble with my radio show, so this needed to work.

Holly and Artie were behind me as I knocked on the door. Mrs Birchem, a truly scary-looking woman, opened it.

'Hello, you again,' she said flatly, eyeing me, then Artie and Holly, and I could've sworn she smiled slightly. Her puckered mouth moved maybe 0.1 millimetres.

'Yes, sorry, our football has gone into your garden – mind if we have a look for it?' I said in a very innocent way that I hoped would not translate as 'I'm very guilty of a grievous cat crime and I'm hiding your stolen cat under here.'

'Why don't you come on in, then?' she said in a rather sinister way. We followed her through the house. Something wasn't right. I could just sense it.

Holly could clearly smell a rat too, as she nudged me and nodded her head. We arrived in the old woman's small kitchen, where a cat bed lay empty, with used cans of cat food everywhere. The place stank. The sooner we got out of here, the better.

'Why don't you all sit down?' she said, as she sat down at the kitchen table. A ball of wool and two knitting needles were in front of her. 'I can make you three a nice glass of orange squash or perhaps a tuna sandwich?'

'Oh no, thank you, Mrs Birchem, we have to be going now . . . once we've . . . er . . . found the football . . .' I said quickly.

She didn't answer and it felt like minutes passed in silence. You could have heard a knitting needle drop. Which it did at one point, clanging on the kitchen floor, sticky with cat food and dust.

'I know you have my cat there,' she said finally, without even looking at us. She picked up the remaining oversized knitting needle and pointed it threateningly at the bulging ski jacket I was holding.

Nothing. No one said a word. Artie's stomach responded by gurgling in fear. It spoke for all of us.

'I can explain,' I said nervously.

'You thought I had stolen your precious Mr Bun Nose cat, didn't you, Artie Barker? So you got your friends to rescue it. Very clever. Very bad idea, though. Messing with me and my darling, darling Mr Pickles. How could you think my beautiful Mr Pickles was your ugly fat cake-faced cat?'

'He's not cake-faced! He's just big-boned,' protested

Artie. Mrs Birchem was right, though, Artie's cat looked like there were three other cats in it.

'Whatever you say, dear. I was so upset I called my son. He's a good boy and loves his mummy so he came over here right away. My nice neighbour saw him and told him she'd seen a scrawny red-haired girl and you, Artie, in my back garden. He's a smart man, my son, and luckily he heard your dreadful radio show. He worked out what you'd done.'

My eyes had wandered to a faded framed photo on the kitchen sideboard of Mrs Birchem and what I guessed was her son. At first glance it looked like she was posing next to some kind of poor deformed freak at a circus. My eyes couldn't stop being drawn to the horror of this monstrosity.

Then it hit me. My blood turned to ice when I finally recognised who the man-thing was.

Who her son was.

'Would you like to meet my son, you three? He's here now.'

The kitchen door creaked appropriately as it opened and a foul-breathed man strode in with a crazed look of satisfaction on his face.

'Meet my son, children,' said Mrs Birchem.

And we all looked into the manic, angry face of our evil headmaster. Mr Harris.

CHAPTER 26

The FRANKEN**HARRIS**STEINS

'Well, well, this is nice. If it isn't my three most favouritest pupils in the whole wide world,' said a very pleased-with-himself Fish Face. He stood next to his bug-eyed, psycho mum. What a gruesome twosome they were.

'*Mrs Birchem?*' said Artie, still trying to put it all together.

'Yes, I went back to my maiden name after my husband left me,' she said. 'But my son has always been loyal. My wonder-boy Kenneth here.'

That monster, a wonder-boy? And *Kenneth*?!

'What shall we do with them, Mother? De-cisions de-cisions,' said Fish Face slowly. He was really enjoying himself. I'd never seen him look so happy.

Then, just when I thought this situation couldn't get any worse, in came Martin Harris. Naturally. Wherever his dad was, so was his faithful gormless henchman. Henchboy. Three generations of mutants.

'What's up, losers?' he leered at us. Psycho Nan ruffled his hair playfully. A family of monsters.

'I mean, I should really call your parents, and the police, to report what you did to my poor old mumsy,' said Mr Harris, still rubbing his chin and thinking. 'Oh, you'd be in some very serious trouble, and it all started with that waste-of-space radio show, yet again. I'm guessing Mum and Dad wouldn't be too happy, would they, Spike?' He grinned so hard I thought his face was going to crack.

Martin Harris let out a fake laugh that sounded like an old car trying to start on a cold morning. 'Huh . . . huh . . . huh . . .' Maybe he hadn't learned laughter yet.

Mr Harris continued to smile, obviously modelling himself on those pet sharks of his. 'But I don't think I'm going to do that. In fact, I think I'm going to make you an offer.'

'What kind of offer?' said Holly. She seemed to be unfazed by all of this. Must be that army training – How Not to Be Intimidated by the Enemy. She bent down and fumbled with her shoe and came back up. Now was surely not the time for worrying about shoe-laces?

'I could do . . . nothing,' said Mr Harris. 'I could say nothing. All of this – you stealing my mother's cat – would be our little . . . secret. Sounds good, right?' he said.

Yep, too good. Where's the catch?

'What?' said Martin. 'But they have to pay.'

Mr Harris sighed. 'Patience, Martin,' he said. He turned to us. 'You just have to do one little, teensy-weensy little thing in return for my very very kind offer,' he said.

'What?' I asked dejectedly. Bracing myself for what was about to come.

'You do not enter the Radio Star competition.'

'WHAT?' I said.

'Merit Radio will enter Radio Star; you won't.

Leaving the way open for me to win. Proving, once and for all, my glorious radio show is the best,' he said. He stared directly at me. A sly grin on his face. 'People will come from far and wide to visit the school and ask to meet the obviously brilliant man who runs such a superb institution *and* its amazing radio show. They will probably erect a statue of me to commemorate my leadership.'

His mouth was almost frothing with excitement at his clever plotting.

This was blackmail.

I couldn't say anything. I was dumbstruck.

'Sleep on it, eh,' said Mr Harris. 'Then let me know tomorrow. We'll meet in my office before class.'

'Would anyone like any cake?' asked Mrs Birchem, bug-eyed mother of a foul and fishy son, holding up a very sharp cake knife.

Get me out of here. This had turned into an X-rated horror movie.

None of us said anything. We just stared at her. Who could eat cake at a moment like this?

'Right,' said Mr Harris after a while, putting a restraining hand on his son's shoulder. 'We have to be going now, son. Enough fun and games for one night.' He turned to us. 'Now if you could just let my poor terrified mother have her cat back,' asked Fish Face. All this while his witch of a mum cut him a slice of cake, probably made from her most recent dead husband's body. Get me out of here! Silently, I handed over the cat prison.

No one said anything as we backed out of the kitchen.

CHAPTER 27

Pretty uneventful

We made our way out of the den of death and, once safely outside, we quickly walked away. All this over that flipping cat of Artie's, Mr Bun Face.

'What are we going to do NOW?' cried Artie.

'I have no idea,' I said. Mr Harris had finally won. I didn't have any choice. Ignore him and he would tell my parents – and he was right, they would go berserk. After everything that had happened last time, and now this. They would end the show.

I couldn't enter Radio Star, but it was everything I'd

ever wanted. To be trained by the legendary Howard 'The Howie' Wright. Now I was going to have to sit back and hear someone else – someone evil – win my dream.

This was the worst moment of my life.

I was about to cry.

But Holly, strangely, looked quite cheerful. She patted Artie on the shoulder. 'Don't worry, I have something up my sleeve. Or my trouser leg, more like.'

'Huh?'

'You'll see,' she said. 'This was my whole idea, Spike – rescuing the cat and going to Mrs Birchem's house, so it's my mess to fix. Go home, I've got this.' And with that she skipped off towards her house.

Me and Artie looked at each other. 'What's she up to now?' I pondered.

'I don't know,' said Artie. 'But if anyone can take on Fish Face, it's her.'

'How was your day, my angel?' said Mum when I got back home. She had successfully cornered me as I walked in through the front door of Number 27 Crow Crescent. For once I was grateful for one of her overly strong bear hugs. I felt myself breathe out for the first time in hours. In that little moment, I felt safe.

'Oh, pretty uneventful, Mum,' I said. In a high-pitched voice.

NEWSFLASH

8 DAYS

192 HOURS

11,520 MINUTES

691,200 SECONDS

UNTIL ENTRIES CLOSE FOR RADIO STAR

CHAPTER 28

Blackmail

'Mr Harris wants to see you three in his office,' said Madame Smith, our French teacher, the moment we walked through the school gates. Even she looked worried for us.

'*Bonne chance, mes enfants,*' she called after us. I'm no French language expert, but I think she was wishing us good luck – either that or saying 'fat chance'.

Artie, Holly and I made our way along the corridors. Our footsteps were echoing around the walls and none of us said much.

We arrived at his secretary's desk.

'Go in, he's waiting for you,' said Mrs Hubert. I always felt so sorry for Mrs Hubert. Imagine having to work with that beast of a man all day every day. Sometimes I think she is a robot that he's built. She often just smiles at you blankly when you ask her a question.

I knocked on the door.

'ENTER,' boomed the command from the other side. I opened the door and we went on in.

Fish Face, our beloved headmaster, was sitting behind his desk. Behind him, smiling smugly, stood his son Martin. Cracking his knuckles.

Fish Face leaned back in his giant throne of a chair and put his hands behind his head. 'Sooooo,' he began. 'Have you made a decision? Will you be bowing out of Radio Star?'

'Oh, I don't think so,' said Holly.

This made him suddenly lean forward in his throne. He frowned. I frowned. Artie frowned. Martin didn't frown – I don't think he knew how to.

Holly still hadn't told us her plan. What was she doing?

'Why not?' said Mr Harris.

'Because of this,' said Holly. She took a small tape recorder from her pocket and placed it on the desk. Then she pressed Play.

Mr Harris's voice came tinnily from the little device.

'I could do . . . nothing. I could say nothing. All of this – you stealing my mother's cat – would be our little . . . secret. Sounds good, right . . .'

Mr Harris went white. He reached over and turned it off. 'OK,' he said. 'So, we have something on each other. I could get your show shut down, you could play this . . . Thus, we are in a stalemate. I won't tell the police about you stealing my mum's cat, and you keep this to yourself. I assume you have copies?'

Holly nodded.

'What?' said Martin. 'Make them pay, Dad!'

'They have a recording of *blackmail*, you cretin,' said Mr Harris. 'If anyone heard that, I would be—'

'Fired instantly?' said Holly.

'Um, yes. Not good. I don't want this to be heard, ever. It's not to protect myself, you understand, I was just joking with some of my favourite pupils, really. You know me, always up for laughs,' he said, smiling a fake smile, some of the colour returning to his cheeks. 'But this recording could be *misunderstood*, it could damage this wonderful education establishment. The children who look up to me would be . . . confused.' He was scratching the side of his neck furiously.

'So we forget all about the blackmail,' said Holly.

'A joke, really, not blackmail,' said Mr Harris in a fake light-hearted manner. Like a robot who had downloaded the "human" program and it had a bug in it.

'Blackmail and no disguising it,' said Holly. 'People will know that. We do nothing with our recording of you, Mr Harris, and you do nothing about the cat incident. The *Secret Shed Show* enters Radio Star.'

Mr Harris closed his eyes and breathed deeply through his nose, flaring his nostrils/gills.

'OK,' he said quietly. Seeing as he was so agreeable, I seized my moment.

'And no more litter-picking for me,' I said.

His eyes widened, and his crocodile mouth snapped open. 'Absolutely not,' he said, slamming his desk with a fist. 'Spike is on litter duty for the rest of his years at school.'

Holly smiled. 'Fine. Then we release the recording . . . and I tell everyone why Martin got kicked out of Army Cadets.'

Now it was Martin's turn to go white. 'NO! Dad . . .' he said.

'You can't,' said Mr Harris to Holly. 'You signed an agreement!'

'Compared to the blackmail, I don't think anyone will care,' said Holly.

'OK!' yelled Mr Harris. 'OK, you win.'

'I know,' said Holly.

'Off you go, then,' said Mr Harris, through gritted teeth. 'I'll keep this.' He took the voice recorder, placed it in a drawer and locked it.

'Sure, help yourself, Mr Harris, because as you said – I've got copies,' said Holly as we started to file out.

'Spike Hughes, can I have a quick word?' said Mr Harris. I nodded to Artie and Holly to carry on without me.

Mr Harris put his sweaty fish paw on my shoulder and leaned in close. Too close. I could smell the coffee breath. It was so strong it could've stripped wallpaper. He began whispering, like a psycho.

'Your friend saved you, Spike Hughes. You got lucky. Mark my words, you will screw up again. You can't help yourself. Hear me now: I will be there when you do and it will be glorious. Run along now . . . *Radio Boy.*' He licked his lips. 'Or should I say "On-borrowed-time Boy!" Tick . . . tock . . . until the next time,' he bellowed after me.

Out in the corridor, I caught up with Holly and Artie.

'You're a genius,' I said to Holly. 'But how did you record him?' I was remembering how she'd stooped to adjust her laces at Mrs Birchem's house, which must have been when she turned something on.

She shrugged. 'I recorded him on my phone, then put it on to my dad's tape recorder. Action, Spike. Action beats inaction. Classic army teaching.'

'And Martin was in the Cadets with you?' I asked.

'Yep.'

'So . . . why *did* he get kicked out?' said Artie.

'I can't tell you, honestly,' said Holly. 'I had to sign something his dad's lawyers gave me. And there was an industrial cleaning team involved too that had to be sworn to silence. Awful business.

The screams will always stay with me.' She stared off into the distance at the memory of the incident that could not be discussed. What a family of monsters.

CHAPTER 29

Lasagne

'You're making *lasagne* in cookery class *today*?!' Mum yelled on Monday morning when I handed her a crumpled-up bit of paper from the bottom of my school bag that I was meant to give her several days before. 'How on earth am I supposed to find fresh parmesan at seven o'clock in the morning? This isn't good enough, Spike!' she complained as she opened and slammed various kitchen cupboards and doors.

Within a few minutes, though, she'd worked her magic. Who needs fresh parmesan when you have some mouldy cheddar at the back of the fridge?

'Thanks, Mum,' I said sheepishly as she handed me a large plastic box with everything in.

'Be careful when you fry your onions not to get too near the naked flame,' she warned.

Great advice, Mum. I hadn't thought of that and had fully intended to cook my own flesh. Fact is, the only danger in that cookery class was from my cooking. I was terrible.

The cooking class was first lesson, and our extremely miserable teacher, Mrs Cankle, told us to get all our ingredients out. We were assembled round the various kitchen units and ovens and I was with Artie and Holly. Unsurprisingly, Artie was a very good chef and food mattered to him. For Artie, the cooking of a lasagne was serious business. Mrs Cankle often asked Artie questions during lessons, not to check he was paying attention, but to check *she* had got it right.

Martin Harris was opposite us, with Katherine Hamilton next to him. To my jealous eyes they looked like some happily married couple cooking together. But from the beginning of that lesson Martin only had eyes for Holly – and not in a good way. Clearly, Holly laughing at his awful feature, *Martin's Minute*, and talking about whatever he'd done at Cadets to get him fired, had really got to him. But there wasn't a chance to warn her about his evil eyes, as Mrs Cankle was shouting at me.

'Why haven't you started making your sauce yet, Spike?'

'Uh, oh yes, sorry, Mrs Cankle,' I said.

'Artie, what's the best temperature for a lasagne to cook in the oven?'

'One hundred and eighty degrees for around forty-five minutes. Until the top is bubbling and lightly browned.'

'There you are, everyone. Do what Artie just said,' said Mrs Cankle.

We had all built our lasagnes as best we could, but Artie's was of course singled out as showing how they should look before we put them in the oven. Mine did not look anything like Artie's intricately layered masterpiece. Mine looked like someone had sat on it. Repeatedly.

'Put them into the ovens now, VERY CAREFULLY!' ordered Mrs Cankle.

Then Mrs Cankle said she had to leave the classroom kitchen for a few minutes, so we should use that time to wash up. I began filling the sink with hot water as Mrs Cankle foolishly left the class all alone.

'We haven't got any tea towels,' noticed Holly.

'They live in the supply cupboard,' Artie said.

'I'll go and get some,' said Holly.

I didn't see what happened next, but I suddenly became aware of some commotion, and then screaming and thumping sounds. I looked around to see Martin Harris laughing to one side of the supply cupboard door. He had the key in his hand.

The revolting mutant ape of a boy had locked Holly in! He'd been watching her the whole time and waiting for his moment of revenge. Now he had it. Holly was kicking the door from within the supply cupboard. I knew, though, that it would just be a matter of time before she had improvised a paperclip and a coathanger to pick the lock and let herself out. Martin would sure be in trouble then.

But time passed and it didn't seem to be happening.

Then, a moment later, I could hear her shouting in there.

And . . . was she *crying*?

I was stunned. She couldn't be. She was invincible. What was going on?

'Let her out, Martin,' I yelled. Katherine Hamilton was cackling like a witch behind him. For the first time ever, I hated her. *This* was the girl I was going to marry? Well, those wedding plans were definitely off.

'Make me,' he said defiantly, puffing his chest out like the ape boy he was. I was no Sensei Spike, so that wasn't about to happen. Instead, it was Artie who sprang into action. Flew into action would be more accurate.

He picked up a large baking tray and, using it as a battering ram, ran at full speed towards Martin Harris. This was now an impromptu lesson in physics for the whole class to enjoy. Artie's size, plus considerable speed, was more than a match for Martin. Artie and the non-stick baking tray rammed into him like a human wrecking ball, sending both of them sailing across the classroom.

The pair bounced off a chair and landed with a thud on top of one of the tables, with Artie, still armed with the trusty baking-tray shield, on top of Martin. The supply cupboard key flew out of Martin's hand

and, as if by divine intervention, landed at my feet.

The rest of the class stood open-mouthed in shock at what they had just witnessed.

It wasn't over yet.

Unfortunately, the table Martin and Artie landed on had all of the yet-to-be-cooked lasagnes sitting

on it. With a loud crack, the table slowly gave way under the weight of lasagnes+Martin+Artie+baking tray and as they hit the floor, they were showered with creamy cheese sauce, followed by a layer of mince, topped off with pasta and a sprinkling of parmesan cheese.

I ran to the supply cupboard door and fumbled in desperate panic to free Holly, who was sobbing inside.

'It's OK, I've got the key!' I shouted. I flung the door open. On the floor next to a large rack with various kitchen utensils, I found Holly, her knees drawn up into her chest.

I heard a noise and turned. Behind me, Martin Harris limped up, grinning – even though he was covered in lasagne sauce.

'You see, Holly,' he said, 'you're not the only one who remembers Cadets. And what *I* remember is how you freaked out when we had to crawl through that tunnel.'

I turned to him, nearly ready to punch him. 'Go away, Martin,' I hissed.

He winked. 'For now,' he said as he walked off.

'Holly, it's OK,' I said gently as I crouched down in front of her. 'But what's Martin talking about?'

'The thing is . . . I'm . . . um . . . terrified of small spaces, Spike,' she said. She couldn't even look me in the eye.

'Well, it's OK now,' I said. 'You're safe.'

'Thanks,' she said. She looked down. 'I'm just . . . embarrassed.'

'I wouldn't want to be shut in here,' I said, looking around. It was like a prison cell. It was packed with bowls of all sizes and enough washing-up liquid to wash every plate in the world several times over.

'I feel so stupid,' she said under her breath.

'Why? He shouldn't have done it. No wonder you got upset.'

'I don't like being weak,' she said, staring ahead at the wall.

'Well, I think you are the strongest and bravest person I know! A karate champion, a rescuer of stolen cats – OK, bad example as it was the wrong cat, but you know what I mean. Everyone's scared of *something*. If you didn't have some fear, you wouldn't be human. You'd be like Martin Harris.'

At that, she smiled weakly.

I don't know why I did this, but I felt it was the right thing to do: I put my hand on Holly's. Mine was warm and hers was icy cold. I let mine warm hers up for a few seconds.

We looked at each other.

This slightly confusing moment with Holly was interrupted by Mrs Cankle's hysterical scream when she walked back into the classroom to find the lasagne explosion.

Then, a moment later:

'YOU POOR GIRL!' shouted Mrs Cankle as she burst into the store cupboard.

Martin Harris was sent immediately to the headmaster's office. Mrs Cankle would never have doubted Artie the master chef's word on what had occurred while she left the class unattended for just three and a half minutes.

I would have loved to have been in that room to hear Fish Face tearing his own son to shreds. I could hear it now: no doubt banging on about 'bringing shame to the family name'.

That afternoon after school, it wasn't me on litter-picking duty. It was Martin Harris. The school's grounds had never looked so clean.

I looked over at Holly as Martin passed us, in his high-visibility jacket and with a small piece of lasagne still stuck to the back of his head.

We both laughed.

Holly turned to me. 'You don't think, like, less of me since what happened earlier?' she asked.

'No.' I grinned at her. 'At least now I know you're human. I wasn't ever entirely sure.'

'Ha ha.' She punched me in the arm. It hurt quite a lot.

Back to the old Holly.

CHAPTER 30

The CHA-CHA CHAT SHOW

When I got back home from school, a strange sight greeted me. My mum was lying flat out on the floor of the lounge. I dropped my school bag and ran to her, immediately fearing she had finally collapsed from too much talking to her mum friends, without taking adequate breaths. She undoubtedly holds the world record for longest telephone call with the least amount of oxygen intake.

Upon closer inspection I saw she was actually moving and fully conscious, busy following an exercise DVD on the TV. But what exercise benefits can you possibly get from lying on your back, thrashing your arms and legs around like an upside-down beetle in distress?

Grandad Ray had obviously heard me come in, and leaped down the stairs to find me and Beetle-Mum in the lounge.

'Good for you, Carol. Gotta stay in shape. I'm as fit as a fiddle,' he said. He then dropped down to the floor himself and started doing press-ups. He'd got no further than three when he asked me to help him up.

'Already did a hundred earlier, so must've overdone it,' said an out-of-breath Grandad Ray. *Sure you did, Topper.*

'I've got homework to do,' I said.

'Did . . . my . . . first . . . radio . . . show . . . the other day, you know,' said Grandad Ray in between panting breaths.

'Oh yeah, did you?' I lied, knowing full well he had, and the 'homework' I had to do was actually listening back to it.

'Yeah and, gotta say, kid, I was a natural. No offence to you, young man, but I think grown-ups make proper radio.'

'Glad it went well, Grandad. Have you heard from Nan recently?' I said sweetly.

'No . . .' said Grandad Ray as he skulked off. *Gotcha.*

'Go easy on him, Spike. He's having a tough time,' urged Mum while her workout show demanded she get up and do star jumps.

'He's doing a radio show at the same time as me, Mum, ON PURPOSE. I'm having a tough time of it too,' I shouted.

Mid-star jump, Mum managed to get out, 'It . . . won't last . . .'

I went to my bedroom to have a secret listen to Grandad's show. I found my headphones and pressed Play. As I listened, I made notes in my notepad. I'm happy to share them with you here on these pages.

Show opens with my Grandad Ray screaming 'WELCOME TO THE GREATEST RADIO SHOW ON EARTH'.

Some women start clapping and screaming. They may be drunk or just insane. Or both.

Some ballroom-type music plays so loudly I immediately move my headphones away from my ears to stop me going deaf.

'Welcome, one and all,' says Grandad Ray. 'My name is Toni Fandango and this is the Cha-Cha Chat Show, with me and the dancing divas . . . Ladies, introduce yourselves . . .'

'Hi, I'm Susan,' purrs one of the dancing divas.

'I'm Jackie,' mumbles someone who sounds either like they are jet-lagged or have been at the wine.

'And my name is DAPHNE,' shouts the last tone-deaf

It was interesting that Grandad Ray wasn't using his real name, no doubt stealing inspiration from my Radio Boy name. Bring it on, Fandango!

'This show is for us older folk, the forgotten generation. Well, we have something to say and we will be heard. We will talk about ballroom dancing and the good old days.'

Oh no, time for a song from Grandad Ray's – or should I say Toni Fandango's – greatest hits. Or misses.

'Those were the DAYZZZZZZZZ, my friend . . .'

The 'song' ends. Rather awkwardly, Grandad Ray

to improve your bossa nova, but now here's a list of twenty things that used to be better in the good old days:

'One. Phones. These mobiles you see young 'uns staring at the whole time. Rubbish. A landline was all we needed and we still managed to beat Hitler and win a World Cup. And invent gravy.*

'Two. Music. The bands we grew up with used to look smart; now it's some kid called Justin Bibber or something with his jeans halfway down his legs and his bum showing for all the world to see. Tuck your bum in, young man! Looks like a kid who's up past his bedtime. Rubbish.

'Three. The weather.'*

I wish I could tell you 3–19, but I fell asleep. I woke up again to:

' . . . finally at twenty. Kids. Much better years ago. Polite, respected older people like us as being wise. Nowadays kids are rude and evil. Fact.'

This goes on for some time, and I switch off for a bit. I think I doze through the bossa nova tips too. The next thing I know, Grandad Ray is wrapping up the show.

'Well, I hope you can join me and the dancing divas

* Grandad Ray loves gravy. So much so I think his blood might be gravy.
* How was the weather better years ago? Why did the people in old black-and-white photos look so miserable, then?

again same time next week. Ladies, say bye . . .'

'See ya,' says Susan. I think.

'Can you wake up Jackie and Daphne,' Grandad tries to say under his breath, but microphones are sensitive and pick up the quietest of sounds.

Ha.

Nothing to worry about there.

NEWSFLASH

4 DAYS

96 HOURS

5,760 MINUTES

345,600 SECONDS

UNTIL ENTRIES CLOSE FOR RADIO STAR

CHAPTER 31

Bring on the red carpets

'I'll give you a lift to school if you like,' Dad offered at breakfast on Tuesday morning.

'Yes, please,' I said. I was hardly going to say, 'Oh, no thanks, Dad, I'd prefer to walk so I can enjoy the feeling of rain on my back and the weight of half the school library crushing my spine,' was I?

Of course I didn't realise then the bombshell he was about to drop on me.

A free ride with Dad was a massive treat. We got in

his car and I immediately turned the radio on to Kool FM and Howard 'The Howie' Wright's breakfast show. He was talking about some of the entries for Radio Star.

'You got your homework?' asked Dad as he guided his heap of a car along our road. Maintaining stock levels of toilet roll and supervising grumpy checkout ladies obviously didn't pay enough for shiny new cars.

'Shhhhhh,' I said. I was listening to Howard talking.

'. . . *some entries are already coming in for Radio Star . . . but remember: you only have three days left to enter . . .*'

Dad reached over and turned it down.

'Dad! I was listening to that,' I cried out.

'I want to talk to you. You already know about the competition, Spike. Can I just ask you why you want to enter?' asked Dad.

'Why? *Why?*' I shouted, a bit hysterically. How could he not understand *why*? Had some washing powder fallen off a top shelf at his supermarket and hit him on the head? 'Because I want to be a proper DJ and this could be my chance. To show people how GREAT I am. People will finally know I'm, like, the real deal. That I'm not just some kid in a shed.'

'You are the *real deal* and already doing a great show. Winning this competition won't change that. I mean, that's if you manage to win, and that's a big if,' said Dad.

'Why is it a big if? Thanks for the vote of confidence, Dad!' I said. Maybe I should've walked to school.

'That's not what I meant, Spike. I think you're amazing, but talent competitions aren't always about who's the best. The person that wins often isn't the most talented. Look at the singers and bands who've won *X Factor*, then look at the ones who didn't – they often go further,' he said.

'Howard "Howie" Wright is a true professional and a fan of mine! He gets it. He will want me to win,' I said.

'Then what, Spike? What changes?' asked Dad.

'EVERYTHING! I'll be really properly famous and everyone will know who I am. Life at school will change overnight. It would be huge. Life-changing,' I said.

Dad sighed, hard. This was also a sign he was thinking. Like he needed to get air out of him for his brain to work. The car window almost misted up, he sighed so much.

'Son, you know who you sound like?' asked Dad.

'Someone who wants to win? A winner?' I asked.

'Grandad,' Dad said.

'NO, I DO NOT!' I yelled back.

'OK, sorry, maybe that's a bit harsh – but all that talk of being famous sounds very familiar to me. Just wanting to win to get more famous isn't good, Spike,' said Dad. 'Obviously, I don't know what it's *like* to be famous, but from what I can see in Mum's magazines, becoming a celebrity promises a lot but it doesn't solve the problems you think it will. Unless you think true happiness is standing on a red carpet with a fake grin. It won't change who you are, Spike, or make you happier. That's not how life works. You do a great show and you've only just started learning what you can do and how good you could really be. Enjoy the journey.'

'In this car?' I asked.

'No! I mean enjoy where you are right now. Doing your shed show, having fun with your mates. Take time to appreciate what you already have.'

'Then why are you entering *Search For a Star,* then? You're a failed rock star,' I said.

'That's it, though. I never even got to be a failed one! I stopped, I gave up. I'm doing it for some fun, Spike.

Just for the fun. You know what the highlight of my day running the supermarket is? Checking the stock levels of toilet rolls. We aren't going to *win*. I doubt we'll even get past the live auditions on Saturday.'

I whipped my head round. 'On *Saturday*?' I'd known it was happening, but I'd been trying to blank it out.

'Yes, why?'

Oh, nothing, Dad, just the end of any status I might have had at school. It hardly bears thinking about. Dad and the Pirates, on national TV.

'Nothing,' I mumbled.

'So you see,' continued Dad, oblivious to the impending death of my school cred, 'it's just for the experience, the fun. Me and the band, we're not doing *Search For a Star* to try and win it. You need to think like that about Radio Star.'

I wasn't really listening any more, as I'd suddenly noticed Martin Harris and Katherine Hamilton walking hand in hand to school.

Katherine would *definitely* notice me if I won Radio Star – though obviously I would ignore her, in revenge for her laughing at Holly. I would be a star. Not just a kids' DJ in a shed. I'd be a real super-star DJ and even the humiliation of Dad being on TV dressed as a pirate couldn't touch me, then.

I started to daydream. In my fantasy I was walking down the school corridor and as I strode purposefully along, people's heads were turning when I passed. *'That's him, Spike Hughes. He won Radio Star,'* they would all say. Girls would run up to me asking for selfies, leaving behind their jealous boyfriends – especially ones called Martin Harris.

'Spike! Spike! Hello, anyone in?' I could hear the words, but I was still in my alternate celebrity world.

'Sure I'll sign your bag, Katherine – uh, sorry, what?' I mumbled as I came back to reality to find my dad looking at me like I'd gone mad.

'*"I'll sign your bag, Katherine"*?' asked Dad, looking confused.

'Sorry, just erm . . . practising a line from the school play we are working on,' I said, far too quickly.

'OK, take it easy, son. Talk more later. Don't forget your bag and have a good day. I love you,' said Dad.

'Love you too, Dad,' I said. As Dad pulled away, the brakes were squealing. I did love my dad, so much, but I didn't want to end up like him. I'd have a sports car, the ones you see with no roof. Not an old banger.

And when I won Radio Star, I *also* wouldn't be wearing a tie with the name of a supermarket on it.

CHAPTER 32

Embarrassing parents

'My parents are world champions at embarrassing me,' I said into my microphone on Wednesday evening's show. 'I mean, my dad's going to be on *Search For a Star* on Saturday. He's in a pirate-themed rock band and their signature song is 'Pirate Party in My Pants'. It's going to be the armageddon of embarrassment.'

'Mine are pretty bad too,' said Artie.

'How?' I asked.

'Remember our school Christmas nativity play? My

dad fell asleep and started snoring so loudly no one could hear what the three wise men were saying,' said Artie.

Holly and I laughed as we remembered it. More people had been watching Artie's dad snoring than our play. People were filming him and taking pictures.

'Well, at least your dad isn't about to embarrass you on national TV.'

'Oh, come on,' said Holly. 'He's in a rock band. It's cool.'

'*Cool?*' I echoed.

Artie leaned into his microphone. 'Spike has a point here, Holly. The potential for embarrassment is very high.'

'Great, thanks, Artie,' I said. 'Anyway, tonight on the *Secret Shed Show*, I want to hear how your parents have embarrassed you. I need to know I'm not the only one struggling.' After I gave out the usual ways they could get in touch, I played a song. Artie had picked it especially because it related to what we were talking about tonight. 'Parents Just Don't Understand' by DJ Jazzy Jeff & the Fresh Prince. A rap song from the late 80s about parent trouble. Might be old, but it was still good.

It seemed we had hit a bullseye with our listeners. I guess all parents are embarrassing; maybe they are just born that way. Sad, really. Could they get any medical help for this? Some tablets maybe?

Doctor: 'What's the problem?'

Patient: 'I'm really embarrassing my children all the time.'

Doctor: 'Don't worry! You're the fifth person I've had in here today with this condition; take these three times a day and if they don't work, maybe leave your family and go and live in the woods.'

'Caller ready to go, Spike,' shouted Holly. The song was ending.

'Hi, it's Radio Boy on the *Secret Shed Show*, taking your calls about your embarrassing parents. Hello, caller – who is this?'

'It's Shane. Hi, Radio Boy and the gang,' said our caller.

'What have your parents done, Shane?'

'I have a twin brother and since we were born, right up until last year when we were ten, they would dress us in matching outfits. In every photo we look so creepy.'

'That's awful, Shane,' I said while laughing.

'Hi, you're on the air. Who is this?' I asked the next caller.

'Hi, Radio Boy. Hi, Artie,' said our new caller, who I could tell was a girl from her voice. I'm observant like that.

'Well, hello,' said Artie, adjusting his hair despite this being radio.

'Can I just say I love your voice, Artie,' she said. Artie's eyes bulged.

'Well . . . well . . . thanks,' stammered Artie.

'Do you have a girlfriend?' asked his female admirer.

'N-n-no I don't, yet,' mumbled Artie, blushing.

'Would you like one?' she asked.

'Right, this isn't a dating show. What's your name?' I asked, trying to steer the show back under my control.

'Suzi, with an i,' she said. I knew this girl, she was in our year.

'Well, Suzi, how did your parents embarrass you?' I asked. Still irritated she hadn't said anything about *my* voice. Maybe my microphone was playing up.

'My dad's disgusting. When I have friends over he makes his bottom "talk" by breaking wind.'

Artie laughed hard – too hard. I couldn't believe how he was behaving. 'What a funny, funny story, really funny story. Great one, wasn't it, Spike?' said Artie.

'Not bad,' I muttered.

Suzi hadn't finished, though.

'Meet me at lunch break by the science block, if you like, Artie,' she offered. Well, this blew Artie's tiny cake-filled mind.

'Yes, yes, interesting,' was all he could say. Artie had got a *girlfriend* from the show. Unbelievable! I really *needed* to win Radio Star. This shed was holding me back and now affecting my love life.

We took another caller.

'Hi, Radio Boy, my mum gets all these embarrassing photos of me out all the time. Like one of me when I was two, naked, wearing only a Santa hat.'

'Brutal,' I said. Why did our mums want to share those embarrassing photos with everyone? Didn't we have rights?

Right then a text appeared on my phone. From Dad.

Dad

I have to go out ASAP.
Your sister is in charge...

As I read the next sentence I couldn't quite believe my eyes.

'You OK, Spike?' asked Artie. We were still live on air and I had gone silent.

'Yeah. Turns out, it's not just parents who embarrass us. Grandparents do too . . . My Grandad Ray has just been arrested,' I said to a stunned Artie and Holly.

And all our listeners.

CHAPTER 33

Duelling dancers

'I know as much as you do,' protested my older sister. We were waiting in the living room. We'd ended the show early on the bombshell news of Grandad's arrest, and Artie and Holly had left to go home.

Holly said she was going to have a go at editing our ten-minute Radio Star entry, taken from all the best things we had done on the show. From the highly illegal cat hunt, and some of our best callers, to the show when we'd caused a Christmas-present explosion, and our embarrassing parent phone-in.

Except right now, it was embarrassing *grand*parents who were most on my mind.

'You *must* know more – how on earth does an elderly man, our grandad, get arrested? Unless it's for crimes against music,' I said.

'Well, as you learned the hard way, Spike, he likes winding people up. I don't know why you let him get to you about that silly DJ competition. I wouldn't bother entering Radio Star if I were you,' said Amber.

'Why not?' I asked.

'Grandad Ray will win. Those dumb competitions love crazy old people,' said Amber in a very matter-of-fact way. Totally unaware she was annihilating my dreams.

'And cute kids,' I emphasised desperately. I had to keep the dream alive. Cute kids surely always beat crazy oldies? Did I still count as a cute kid?

'But he's a crazy old guy who can also sing and dance. He's like a grandad Swiss Army knife,' she said. She had me there: dream back to total annihilation.

'Well, we'll see, I'm pretty sure his entry will be total rubbish compared to mine,' I said. I thought back to the secret recording of the Dancing Divas and their on-air snoozes.

Suddenly we heard the sound of squealing brakes outside the house. Dad's rust-bucket of a car was back, crash-landing by the sound of it. We could see Grandad the criminal in the front seat. Amber and I had rushed over to the lounge window. We saw Dad turn the engine off, and get into a very animated conversation with Grandad Ray. I was no lip reader, but their conversation definitely contained a few swear words. Dad even slammed his hand on to the steering wheel, which made the car-horn bleat, like a poorly goat.

'Oh my goodness, Spike! You won't believe this, but Grandad Ray has a black eye,' said Amber.

'What? I thought tonight was his ballroom lesson, not boxing! How did he . . .' As my words trailed off, Amber and I had exactly the same thought.

'You don't think he got into a fight at his ballroom lesson, do you?' I said.

The front door opened and in traipsed a very sheepish-looking Grandad Ray. He did indeed have a very swollen black eye.

'Hi, kids,' said Dad, trying to sound all normal and not like he'd just walked in with a heavyweight boxing loser. He blew out his longest sigh ever. 'Grandad err . . . erm . . . had a misunderstanding with another gentleman at tonight's ballroom-dancing class. The police were called and it's all OK now.'

'I was physically assaulted by a complete thug,' burst out Grandad Ray. His trademark golden necklace was broken in his hands.

'Apparently you were dancing in an ungentlemanly fashion with his wife; a tango too far, according to witnesses,' said Dad, with his hands on his hips like he does when he is telling us off. It must be great when you get to be a grown-up and can start telling your parents off. Can you send them to bed early? Or ground them?

'How was I to know her husband was a member of that idiotic postman Senator Terry's karate club?' said Grandad Ray.

'SEN-SEI,' I corrected him.

'Whatever. Psychopaths in pyjamas, if you ask me. He got a lucky punch in, that's all,' said Grandad Ray.

'Apparently you tried to hide from him behind some of the ladies,' Dad said, not quite succeeding in suppressing a smirk.

'LIES!' protested Grandad Ray.

With that he looked up and widened his stance,

gazing into the distance. Oh no, time for a song . . .

'DON'T . . . STOP . . . BEEEEEEEEELIEVVVVVVING.'

'OK, enough excitement for one night. Carol will be home any minute now and will have a look at your eye. Bedtime, you two,' said Dad, nodding at me and my sister.

My grandad had been in a fight and got himself arrested. This was no time for sleep. Mum came in the front door then, just back from her Zumba class.

'For crying out loud, WHAT ON EARTH has happened to Ray's face?' she said in a far-from-calm voice.

She looked accusingly at my dad, then me, and then back at my dad again. As if Dad or me were the main suspects for giving Grandad the black eye.

'Grandad Ray had a little *misunderstanding* at tonight's ballroom-dancing club,' said Dad.

'And the police arrested him,' added Amber helpfully.

'You should see the other guy,' said Grandad Ray.

'Really?' said Dad.

Grandad hung his head. 'Well . . . no,' he said and sloped off to bed. My bed.

NEWSFLASH

2 DAYS

48 HOURS

2,880 MINUTES

172,800 SECONDS

UNTIL ENTRIES CLOSE FOR RADIO STAR

CHAPTER 34

NEVER MEET your HEROES

But wait.

Scratch that. The next morning brought major breaking news.

NEWSFLASH

0 more days until handing in *my* entry because . . .

Today was the day.

We were handing in our entry for Radio Star.

Holly had texted me that morning. She'd finished editing our entry. As soon as she emailed over a link I downloaded it and listened. Wow. I didn't want to be too boastful, but this entry rocked. The judges would have no option but to give me – I mean, us – the win.

I didn't want to risk losing the CD in the post, so I was going to personally deliver it by hand. I set my alarm extra early so I could cycle to Kool FM's studio on the way to school. It wasn't much of a detour for this very important package.

Dad was already in the kitchen making his breakfast and looked shocked to see me up so early.

'Wow! What happened – you wet the bed?' This was what I would call a classic 'Dad joke'. No one laughs at these – only him. This 'you wet the bed?' one is made every time I get up early. *Every. Single. Time.*

Other classic Dad jokes are:

1. If I ever leave a door open, we get 'You born in a barn?' I don't understand this. If indeed I was born in a barn, why would I prefer to leave doors open? Surely the barn animals of

various kinds would escape? I don't see many barns where I live, but whenever I do they seem very shut to me.

2. Any time I accidentally trip over, I hear 'Enjoy your trip! Send us a postcard.' Again, makes no sense. Why would I send anyone a postcard from the place I tripped over? What would I say?

Hi Nan,
Wish you were here! On this pavement outside Mr Kleen the dry-cleaner's where I've just tripped over. Weather is pretty horrid.
Lots of love, Spike xxx

I just hope none of this 'funny' comes out during Dad's TV audition this weekend on *Search For a Star*.

'No, Dad, I haven't wet the bed, thanks. I'm dropping off my Radio Star entry,' I said, pouring the milk on my cereal.

'Great. Good luck. In that case, you can do me a favour and drop this one off as well,' he said, and passed me an envelope.

'What's that?' I asked.

'Your grandad's entry,' he replied.

'One show! He's done one show and it was awful,' I said, stunned at Grandad Ray's arrogance, thinking he had nailed the art of radio in one drunken shambolic show.

'Then you have nothing to worry about, do you?' said Dad.

We said our goodbyes and I headed to Kool FM and my destiny. I got there quickly – an Olympic cyclist would've been proud of my time. I took my bike helmet off and locked my bike up against some railings. I looked up at the radio station. I could see a large aerial on the roof. The building seemed massive. It towered over me. I lost count of the floors it had. At least five.

Plastered all over the window of the reception were posters saying 'KOOL FM – Playing all the Hits'. I pressed the buzzer by the front door, shaking with nerves.

'Hello?' said a lady through the speaker.

'Er . . . Hi. Hello. I'm here with my entry for Radio Star,' I stuttered.

'Come in,' said the speaker. I heard the door unlock and I pushed it open and walked straight into reception. I could hear the news from the speakers that were on the wall. *Speakers on the wall! Radio stations have speakers on the wall!* My eyes widened as I tried to take it all in. I was in an *actual* radio station. Not a shed, a proper radio station. This was an Aladdin's cave to me. I was like Charlie when he first sees Wonka's factory. I glanced towards a large photo of Howard 'The Howie' Wright, pretending to yawn and pointing at an alarm clock. How funny. That Howard was a trickster.

'So you are entering Radio Star,' asked a very smiley receptionist who had bright red lipstick and huge hair.

'Yes. I'm Spike Hughes, Radio Boy. I already do a show,' I said. Wanting to reassure the smiling lady I wasn't just some sad fame-seeking kid giving it a go. I was *already* a DJ.

'Really? My son listens to him,' said the smiley lady.

'That's me. I'm him,' I said.

'You're Radio Boy! Really? Well, wait there, Howie will want to come and say hi, I'm sure,' said Mrs

Smiley (as I will now call her). She picked up a bright red phone, held her hand over the mouthpiece, and whispered to me, 'This goes direct to the studio.'

Radio stations have SPECIAL PHONES THAT GO STRAIGHT TO THE STUDIO. Incredible. One day I will have a special phone. Maybe to go straight to the kitchen so I can get Mum to make a cheese toastie.

I couldn't believe Mrs Smiley was going to ask my hero to come to the place where I was standing. *Stay cool, Spike, stay cool.*

'Oh, hi, studio. Howard, that kid Radio Boy – you know . . . the kid that does a show in a broom cupboard—'

'Shed,' I corrected.

'Sorry, *shed* – he is here in reception. He's got his entry for Radio Star. I thought, as the news and sports was on, you might wanna pop down and say hi quickly . . . What? Does he look . . .'

She spun round in her chair so her back was towards me and started whispering the next bit into the phone. I was just under a metre away, so could still hear. Adults are lousy at whispering. FACT.

'No, Howie . . . he doesn't look mad.'

Did he just ask her if I looked mad?

She hung up and turned round.

'He's coming down. He can't wait to meet you,' she said.

The glass door that went into reception from the radio station flung open and smashed against the wall. Howard 'The Howie' Wright clearly liked to make a grand entrance like my mum.

'The secret DJ! Radio Boy himself!' yelled my hero. He had very white teeth and looked extremely tanned, despite the fact it wasn't summertime. His hair looked perfectly positioned.

He thrust his hand towards me. 'Howard "The Howie" Wright – call me Howie, or "Legend" if you like.' He laughed hard at his own joke. That Howie was such a trickster. What a guy!

'It's a pleasure to meet you, Mr Howie,' I said. I thought I was going to faint.

'I bet,' he said and I wasn't sure if he was joking. 'You're entering Radio Star?' he asked. He seemed surprised.

'Yes, here is my entry. I hope you like it.'

I handed him the best bits of the show on CD and the completed entry form (I've attached a copy at the end of this chapter).

'Why the heck not? A kid on a real radio show . . . it could work . . .' He paused and smiled. 'Big step up from a shed.'

'I'm steady,' I said.

'Steady?' asked Howie, frowning at me.

'Ready, I meant ready,' I said, hating myself.

'Oh, bless him, look at him! He's all nervous to meet you, Howie,' said Mrs Smiley the receptionist. I went bright red. Thanks, Mrs Smiley. Not.

'Wow! You could toast marshmallows on that red face right now, kid,' said Howie, and he laughed hard again at his own joke and patted me on the back. It felt like we were mates now.

'Quick, let's get a photo before I have to head back,' he suggested. I fumbled in my school bag for my phone. I hadn't been expecting to get a picture. I found the phone, but in doing so my lunch box fell out on the reception floor. Howie kindly bent over to help me, but the lunch box fell open and revealed a note from my mum:

Don't forget to eat your apple, my little cutey cutester

Mum xxx

Oh no. I immediately wrote another note in my head. It read:

Dear Ground, please swallow me up.

Howard 'The Howie' Wright saw the note (the one from Mum, not the one in my head). Our eyes met; mine then looked down at the ground in shame. I'd made it weird.

My phone then took ages to turn on, of course. Howie kept looking at his watch.

'I'm gonna have to bolt in a sec, kid, as we're out of news and sport and into a song now,' he said.

COME ON, PHONE, TURN ON, YOU STUPID PIECE OF—

'It's on now,' I said, almost in tears at the full

horror of the last three minutes of my life. I was sweating. Mrs Smiley took my phone.

We posed for a photo, Howie placed his arm over my shoulder and gave this fake grin, then looked at his watch.

'Sorry, kid – I have to go NOW.' He let go of me and walked off, just as Mrs Smiley took the photo. Great.

RadioStar
ENTRY FORM

Name _Spike Hughes_

Age _12_

Address ▮▮▮▮▮▮▮▮▮▮▮▮

▮▮▮▮▮▮▮▮▮▮

▮▮▮▮▮

Why do you think you could win RadioStar?

I already do my own radio show, The Secret
Shed Show. I'm Radio Boy. The ~~world's~~ world's
youngest DJ.

I'm ready to learn from the best. I know ~~how~~ how
all the buttons work so you wouldn't have to train
me ~~up~~ up. I also won't need any food as Mum says
she will provide me with a packed lunch every day.

Pick me. I will be the ~~the~~ best apprentice
to the Master of radio, Howard 'the ~~Howie~~' Hughes.

I have ~~also~~ put a teabag in the envelope
with this application so you can have a nice
cup of tea as you listen to my entry. (I was
going to include a biscuit but was worried
about breakage.) PLEASE PICK ME !

CHAPTER 35

A bad thought

As I closed the door of Kool FM, a devil and an angel were in my head having a major argument.

Angel: 'Hey, Spike, you forgot to hand in your Grandad Ray's entry to Radio Star. You should do the right thing and put it in the station letterbox.'

Devil: 'Or maybe not do that, Spike, and just hang on to it.'

Angel: 'But that's not nice. He's your grandad.'

Devil: 'Who is also trying to stop you winning Radio Star.'

Angel: 'Don't do it, Spike.'

Devil: 'Do it, Spike. PUT IT BACK IN YOUR BAG and forget you've got it.'

Angel: 'You'll feel bad.'

Devil: 'You'll feel just great. Just great.'

I cycled away from Kool FM to school, as if I was fleeing the scene of a crime. In my school bag was Grandad Ray's entry. I *was* going to hand it in for him. Once I'd done something. The devil in me hadn't won completely . . . just a bit.

The thought of it made me smile for the first time that day. Sometimes bad ideas make you smile.

NEWSFLASH

2 DAYS UNTIL I BECOME A LAUGHING STOCK AT SCHOOL AFTER MY DAD APPEARS ON TV IN A BAND. DRESSED AS A PIRATE.

CHAPTER 36

Ninja Dad

'What are you up to?' Dad asked me, making me jump out of my skin.

Sometimes your parents just know when you're doing something you really shouldn't be. And I was.

I took my headphones off and slammed my laptop shut.

'Oh, just some boring homework.'

'Uh-huh, sure,' said Dad. Unconvinced.

He had materialised out of nowhere in my bedroom. Parents can do this. It's one of their mysterious superpowers. It's quite an irritating ability, in my view. The power of appearing when you least want them to.

If my dad was a superhero, I would call him Ninja Dad and he would be the dullest superhero ever.

My dad's superpowers would be:

- the ability to open jam jars easily. Once Mum has already loosened them.
- repelling anyone with the powerful death stink from his backside. Maybe I should call him Fart Man.
- mending the Wi-Fi. By turning it off, then on again.
- the power to always get my friends' names wrong; this also extends to TV shows, actors, singers. Sometimes I need a Google Translate for my dad, to work out who or what he is referring to:

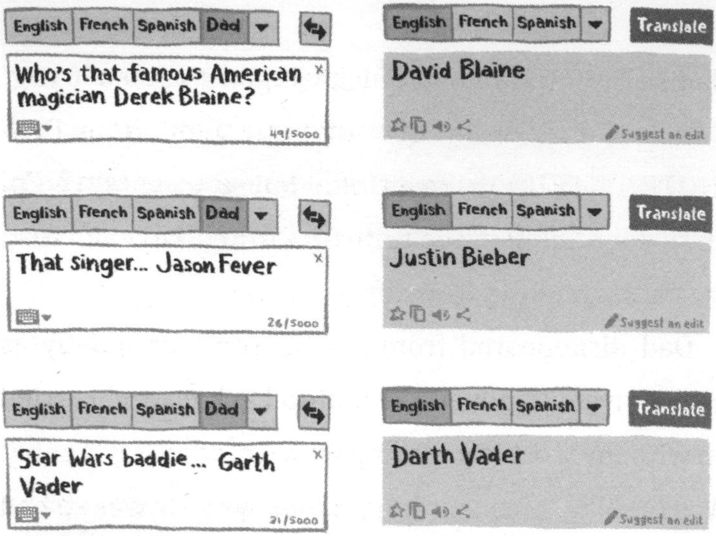
English French Spanish Dad
Who's that famous American magician Derek Blaine?
49/5000
English French Spanish
Translate
David Blaine
Suggest an edit
English French Spanish Dad
That singer... Jason Fever
26/5000
English French Spanish
Translate
Justin Bieber
Suggest an edit
English French Spanish Dad
Star Wars baddie... Garth Vader
31/5000
English French Spanish
Translate
Darth Vader
Suggest an edit

Dad was right, of course; I was up to no good. I was about to sabotage Grandad Ray's Radio Star entry using the audio software on my laptop – just a little bit, the devil had said. I could edit it to make it sound terrible. Even more terrible than it already was.

'I really hope that *is* your homework, son,' said Dad. 'Because if I was to open that laptop up and check, I wonder what I would find.'

'Nothing,' I said. 'Nothing. Honest.'

'Choices, Spike, our life is all about choices. Today's choice is tomorrow's destiny. Sometimes we forget we *have* choices. I hope you are making the right one now, whatever it is you're doing. I can tell by the look on your face you're up to something. Plus anyone who slams a laptop shut that quickly is guilty of something.'

How did he know? Get out of my mind, Ninja Dad! (NOTE TO SELF: make a tinfoil hat to wear when I'm up to something in the future so Ninja Dad can't read my mind and I can be evil.)

Dad disappeared from my bedroom as quietly as he'd arrived. I opened the laptop back up and carried on with my work, tampering with Grandad Ray's entry. Was I really doing anything wrong when it was so bad anyway? Choices, Dad, sure, but what choice did I have? My crazed grandad had made his choice to try to beat his own grandchild in Radio Star.

Right at that moment, Grandad Ray began singing in the shower at the top of his voice . . .some song about a tiger's eye. I've heard it before in a boxing movie called *Rocky*, that my dad always falls alseep in front of at Christmas. We go to change the channel over and Dad wakes up and says 'I was watching that.'

Bouncing back from his black eye, not a care in the world. No sense of guilt at trying to ruin his grandson's future. Unbelievable. Choices, Dad, choices.

I carried on 'editing' his entry. Basically, in just a few minutes I'd made a copy and very quickly altered his voice, to slow it down so he sounded like he was a crazy drunk person.

A text appeared on my phone. From Dad.

Dad

> Hey. Hope you're ok. Choices, son. I think in your heart you understood what I said earlier. Dad x

I looked all around me, above me – was he watching me?

The angel in my head appeared.

Angel: 'You could undo this. It's only a copy. It's not too late.'

Oh! Go away, angel, go away, Dad. Why does it hurt so much to do the right thing?

I hit 'undo'. Then I went back to the original file. In fact, I even tidied Grandad's poxy entry up a bit for him to make it sound better. I balanced the audio a little, taking down the far-too-loud music and bringing the voices up. I cleaned up some room noise and boosted the bass tones to make it less tinny. This is the sort of thing a millionaire record producer does. Polishes poop so it doesn't smell as bad any more.

Now, Grandad's entry sounded almost . . . good.

Why can't I be evil?

I put his entry in an envelope along with his completed entry form. Not before I'd had a sneaky read of it, though.

RadioStar
ENTRY FORM

Name RAY HUGHES (ALSO KNOWN AS TONI FANDANGO, FORMER PROFESSIONAL CABARET SINGER)

Age NONE OF YOUR BUSINESS

Address WHEREVER I LAY MY HAT

Why do you think you could win RadioStar?

STOP THE COMPETITION! YOU HAVE FOUND THE WINNER

I'M A NATURAL ENTERTAINER NOT SOME DESPERATE KID OR WANNABE.

I'VE WON BEFORE, BACK IN 1974 I WAS RUNNER UP IN THE SUNSHINE CRUISE 'STAR OF THE SEAS' COMPETITION WHICH EVERYONE SAID I WON REALLY.

What did he mean, 'desperate kid'? Did he mean me? Because he always writes in capitals, it was quite easy to copy his handwriting so I added something:

> 'STAR OF THE JERS COMPETITION WHICH EVERYONE SAID I WON REALLY.
>
> MY GRANDSON SPIKE HUGHES IS ENTERING THIS AND HE IS WHO YOU SHOULD REALLY PICK AS A WINNER. WOW, HE REALLY IS THE BEST.

I cycled over to Kool FM and dropped off his entry at reception before I had time to change my mind. After leaving the building I looked up at the sky to see if Dad was watching me.

'Happy now?' I shouted up into the sky.

'You OK, Spike?' came a voice behind me.

'Oh, yes, sorry,' I said. It was Howard 'The Howie' Wright. Oh no.

'I was . . . erm, just . . . practising my lines from the school play,' I said, rattling off my now go-to excuse when behaving like a loon.

'Right. Dropping off another entry, I see,' he said.

'Yes, my grandad's,' I said through gritted teeth.

Howie's eyes widened and lit up.

'Your grandad is entering? Against you?'

'Yes, he is,' I replied. Obviously Howie felt sorry for me and was no doubt wondering what kind of grandfather would do such an evil thing.

'FANTASTIC! Oh, the drama,' Howie said, rubbing his hands with glee.

'Gotta shoot, Spike, off to open a new butcher's shop. I'm doing it gratis in exchange for free mince for the rest of the year,' he added, and departed.

That was it, then. Grandad was entered into Radio Star.

NEWSFLASH

4 DAYS UNTIL I FIND OUT IF I'M A FINALIST FOR RADIO STAR. OR MY GRANDAD

1 DAY UNTIL MY LIFE AT SCHOOL BECOMES HELL THANKS TO MY MID-LIFE-CRISIS DAD

CHAPTER 37

Dad's on the TV

D Day. Dad Day. Disaster Day.

Dad On the TV Day. The day what little coolness I had as the school's resident renegade DJ was about to be DESTROYED.

As the morning light crept into my bedroom, I yawned and opened my eyes. Immediately, I shut them again and willed sleep to come back to me so that this day would never start. A giant eraser was poised over my life, about to rub away into oblivion any cool points I'd collected from me being Radio Boy. All this because my dad and the band he used to be in a hundred years ago had thought it would be fun to play a gig in a pub.

Your parents are embarrassing enough, without them dancing and singing on TV in front of millions of people! They should be banned from ever being on TV. My dad once came to pick me up from school in denim shorts, white vest and a baseball cap. He looked like something from an MTV documentary about people who marry their cousins. Weeks after that, the older kids at school, led by Martin Harris, of course, were still talking about my 'Hillbilly Dad'. Thanks, Dad.

When I reluctantly came downstairs, Dad was getting his stuff ready before meeting the rest of his band and heading to the TV studios.

'I'm so nervous, Spike,' he said.

'Yeah, I bet. You don't have to do it, you know . . .' I said hopefully.

Ninja Dad saw through me.

'Oh, I see. Thinking about yourself, Spike, and how it's going to look – your dad on TV? Well, I really want to do this – it's just a bit of fun. I'll try not to embarrass you and ruin your street cred,' he said.

'Good luck, Mr Rock Star,' said Mum as she and Dad hugged.

'Thinking about doing the old stick flick, Carol,' said Dad.

'Be careful! You could have someone's eye out! You're not twenty-one any more,' said Mum.

'Yes, I do know that. Thanks, Carol,' said Dad.

'What song are you doing?' I asked.

'One of our big numbers from back in the day. "Pirate Parade",' said Dad.

I couldn't hold back. 'Pirate Parade?' I asked.

'Yeah, big full-on rock song, huge drum solo from me; it's about being proud of who you are as a pirate and as a person,' said Dad.

Just then Grandad Ray walked in.

'Parade of fools, more like – if you ask me,' he said.

'Well, no one *did* ask you, but thanks for the support, Dad,' said Dad.

Seemed odd, seeing my own dad arguing with his dad. Incredible: even at my dad's old age, you still argue with your parents.

Maybe it starts with arguing with your parents about tidying your room and ends with arguments about which care home you will put them in?

As always, my mum tried to be the peacekeeper. 'I think Grandad was just having a little jokey-wokey,' she suggested.

'Yeah, some people just can't take a joke,' said Grandad Ray, stirring it up.

My dad just did a super-sized sigh and raised his eyebrows as if to make his face into an emoji of 'whatever'. 'Well, I've got to go. Wish me luck, and remember to tune in tonight, 8pm, and vote!' said Dad. He looked really nervous, so we hugged and I even managed to wish him luck.

Dad and Grandad Ray shook hands awkwardly. My mum handed my dad a bag that was bulging at the sides.

'What's in here?' asked Dad as he struggled to hold the bag up to examine its contents.

'Home-made tuna and sweetcorn sandwiches for you and the band, some water, plasters if you get cut, bandages for any muscular injuries, a thermometer, tweezers and some special tablets in case you get the runs like you do when you're nervous,' said Mum with a knowing look.

'Oh no, Mum, please, TMI,' I cried. The thought of my dad losing control of his bodily functions live on TV was too much. I'd have to leave my school and probably the country and/or universe. Maybe start again somewhere like Africa, where no one knew me or about my dad's Pirate Parade and trouser explosion.

Dad left and we all waved him off into his stretch limousine with blacked-out windows. Except it wasn't. It was a boring white mini van he and the band had hired to take them and their equipment to the TV studios. Crammed into the back of a hire van with 'DINGLE VAN HIRE' plastered down the side wasn't exactly living the dream in my view. When I became a famous DJ, I'd have a limo to take me to school.

They did, however, have pirate flags plastered over the van windows.

The rest of Saturday dragged slowly by. Dad called later in the afternoon and said the rehearsal had gone well. Then it was 7.57pm and we all gathered in the front room and waited. Mum, my sister Amber, me, Sherlock and even Grandad Ray, who was pretending to be reading a book. *Radio for Beginners*. Yeah, you really should read that, Grandad.

The theme tune started and then the two hosts were on stage in front of thousands.

'Welcome! What a show tonight! We have a juggler, some gymnasts, dancing dogs and a rock band of dads! Stay tuned.' Then the cameras cut to backstage where I saw my dad.

'THERE'S DAD!' I yelled. Mum screamed, Amber screamed and even Grandad Ray put the book down he was still pretending to read. It took us all a few seconds to take in the sight on our TV screen. Dad and the rest of the band were in their new-for-TV, matching pirate costumes. All silky white pantaloons and plastic sabres.

'Oh no . . .' I said.

Dad had a patch over one eye. Oh dear. Lead singer Tom had a pretend stuffed parrot on his shoulder. They all just looked like they were on the way to a bad fancy-dress party. Now the front room fell silent, except for Grandad Ray, who started laughing very loudly.

'I hope he had his sandwiches and took his tummy pills,' said Mum, concerned.

We watched the dancing dogs, with silky costumes not that different from the band, the triple-jointed

Russians who put themselves into a shoebox, and two elderly gentlemen juggling goldfish bowls. They all did their bits and then the judges gave their thoughts. The main judge was called Simon Scowl. He was a millionaire record producer who, despite all that money, had the worst haircut I've ever seen on a human being. Maybe millionaires don't go to Mr Tops the barber, like my dad, and just cut their own hair. He only buttoned his shirt halfway up too – again, maybe this was a millionaire thing. My dad buttoned his shirts all the way up, but he ran a supermarket not a record label.

As Grandad Ray was nodding off, the hosts introduced the next act. We'd just seen yet another dog, which 'danced' to disco music. Except it didn't really, it just barked a few times, got up on its hind legs, then did a little pee on the studio floor. So the bar was set really high.

'Now, a rock band with a difference. Twenty years ago they almost made it big – now they are a supermarket manager, a tanning salon owner, and an insurance salesman. Please give a big warm welcome to . . . THE PIRATES.'

The audience cheered as the camera swooped up high above and the band started playing. To be fair they weren't that bad, until the singing started. Tanning salon owner Tom shouted at the top of his voice. Like the crazy man we have in town who looks through the rubbish bins and shouts at the moon.

My dad was getting a lot of attention from the cameras due to his crazy drumming. He was actually quite good, which was surprising, but he was grimacing like a loon as he smashed the life out of his drums and cymbals. Then he did the special trick he'd mentioned to Mum this morning. He threw his drumsticks up in the air as the song was coming to an end. Years ago, as a younger, sharper man, this must've really been a crowd-pleaser, as he then would presumably casually catch the drumsticks as they came down to earth.

However, Dad was not that younger man any more.

The drumsticks went up OK, but Dad caught only one as it came spinning back down. The other hit a cameraman on the back of the head, causing him to drop and smash the camera. All of this watched by millions, as the TV screen and what we were watching dropped suddenly to the stage floor and the screen cracked. They cut after a few seconds to another camera. The audience were pointing at the smashed camera lying in pieces on the floor, and laughing. This was turning into car-crash TV.

My dad was having the time of his life and wasn't in the least bothered by what he had just done and carried on drumming with just one stick. He looked the happiest I'd seen him in a long time. I wasn't so happy. But worse was yet to come.

Dad suddenly stood up from his drum stool and kicked over the drums. What was he doing now?

'What's he doing? Sit back down,' yelled Mum, not laughing any more as my dad was mid-rampage. He then ran towards the front of the stage.

Grandad Ray stopped laughing. 'Oh no, son, don't do it,' he said.

'Do what?' I asked.

He didn't have time to reply. Dad ran at full speed to the front of the stage and then launched himself into the air. He *stage-dived.*

'NO! You'll break your neck, you silly fool,' wailed Mum, holding her hands over her mouth in disbelief.

But he didn't. When rock stars stage-dive into the

audience, the adoring fans catch them and pass them around. Held above them by their worshipping hands.

But in all his crazed excitement Dad had forgotten where he was. No adoring audience clamouring to catch you there, Pirate Dad. He launched himself into the air and from a considerable height landed his pirate body on the judges' desk. Immediately cracking it right down the middle. Glasses of water went flying and Simon Scowl leaped out of his chair looking terrified and wet. The audience screamed, in either horror or enjoyment.

The hosts could hardly speak due to the noise the crowd were making, as they gave out the number to text if you wanted the Pirates to go into the semi-finals. The band regrouped, arms round each other, while just in the background you could see a first-aider attending to the injured cameraman Dad had wiped out and a girl dabbing the water from Simon Scowl's face.

The desk collapsed in a heap.

'What was *that*?' said Grandad Ray in shock. Speaking for all of us.

'He'll be a laughing stock,' said Mum quietly.

She reached for the remote and quickly turned the

TV off before the judges could trash Dad. I turned my phone off. I couldn't bear to see any of the messages that were bound to come – laughing at my crazy Pirate fool of a Dad. I plodded up the stairs to my room.

The house was eerily silent, as if in shock.

But the real shock was still to come.

CHAPTER 38

A reluctant star is born

Luckily sleep rescued me and I didn't even hear Dad come in later.

I felt full of fear and dread when I got up and stumbled down to breakfast. I don't know what I expected to see, but it didn't include my dad, grinning from ear to ear, eating his toast. Maybe he would start crying and begging my forgiveness *after* his buttered toast and Marmite?

'We made the semi-finals, son!' he coughed and spluttered.

'*What?*' I said.

'Yeah! The audience loved it. The judges too, once they recovered from the surprise of the, um, broken desk.'

I stared at him, noticing his ribs and stomach were bandaged up.

'War wound from my, er, stage-dive,' he said.

'Back up. You made the *semi-finals*?' I said. Surely he had finally lost his mind? Maybe he'd banged his head on Simon Scowl's massive ego. This just couldn't be true.

'I'm stunned too. We all are,' said Dad in his matter-of-fact way, as if he was discussing the weather or the price of cornflakes in his supermarket.

Finally I plucked up the courage to turn my phone on and read the news about last night's show. It was unbelievable: the public had loved them. My dad's failed drumstick trick and desk-smashing routine had stolen the hearts of the people watching, and they'd won the public vote by a landslide. The public liked seeing them having fun, and it meant the Pirates would be going through to the live semi-final.

My phone didn't stop buzzing with messages sent last night.

Artie

Legend 👍

Holly

OMG! That was the best thing I've ever seen on TV. I voted for him 😄

Turns out I'd been wrong in so many ways. Dad's stage-dive went viral around the world. It was being shared on Facebook and Instagram millions of times. The highlight being judge Simon Scowl's panic-stricken face as my crazed dad dived at him. *What is it with my family? Why can't they just be normal? I thought I was the star. Now I'm competing with my own dad and my grandad. Great.*

Our phone didn't stop ringing all day. Interview offers for Dad from various TV and radio shows. Grandad Ray was irritated. I was too.

'Enjoy it while it lasts, son. There will be some new interweb thing tomorrow, a laughing cat or something,' said a clearly jealous Grandad Ray. He was still on page one of his *Radio for Beginners* book.

But he made an interesting point. I took out the little notebook I carry everywhere for occasions like this, when I see or think of something funny for my radio show. I wrote in it:

Can animals laugh?
I don't think they can.
I've never seen my dog chuckle at, say, a cat falling over.
I might go to the local pet shop later and see if a parrot giggles. Sherlock sighs a lot, but never laughs. Maybe he's just a really serious dog.
I bet cats secretly laugh at their dumb owners behind their backs.

Holly called and suggested we get Dad on the radio show this week. My heart sank at the awful memory of what happened the last time a family member of mine was on the show.

'Your dad is pretty cool and without him we wouldn't have the show. Don't forget it was his idea,' she said.

So I had to go into the kitchen and book my dad as a guest on the *Secret Shed Show*. Something I never thought I'd have to do.

Artie came round to ask my dad if he had any recordings of the Pirates' songs as he'd like to play one on our show that week. From the start I'd let Artie be in charge of all the songs, and for the first time I was regretting it. Unfortunately, my dad *did* have recordings and – hurray – we would get another chance to hear 'Pirate Parade'.

Next day at school, not a single word from anyone about the *Secret Shed Show*, not a peep, even though it was nearly time for The Howie to reveal the shortlist for Radio Star.

Instead, it was all about my now-famous dad. Katherine Hamilton even came up to me and asked ME if I could get HIS autograph.

I hate my life.

CHAPTER 39

The Final Countdown

Today was *my* day.

I'd been awake since 6am – how could anyone sleep when waiting for news like this?

This very morning, Howard 'The Howie' Wright was finally announcing the finalists in his Radio Star competition. Yep, my destiny awaited me. Or did it? I wasn't the only one in the house up early in expectation. The singing in the shower told me Grandad Ray was awake too, obviously thinking his destiny also awaited him. Dream on, old man!

I turned the radio on in the kitchen.

'*Good morning, 6.07am on the big one, Kool FM. Howie here and, folks, what a show today. Win a brand-new mattress thanks to The Bed Warehouse where all this month it's 25 per cent off all beds, plus I announce the four lucky finalists in Radio Star and we find out what they will be doing to try and win the big prize. First, here's Nickelback.*'

Putting aside the fact he'd prioritised giving away a bed over my destiny, this was so exciting. So if I made the final four finalists, then a challenge awaited me? Bring it on, Howie. What could it possibly be? As long as it didn't involve any kind of sport, I would be OK.

Time really drags when you're looking at your watch every few seconds and counting cornflakes. Finally, Howie said, '*Coming up next, the final four in Radio Star.*'

'SPIKE! SCHOOL! NOW!' yelled Mum.

'In a MINUTE, Mum,' I replied. 'Howie is about to announce the results!'

'No, it's SCHOOL TIME. You are going to be late, come on,' said Mum. I grabbed my headphones and opened up Kool FM's app on my phone. I would have to walk to school and listen.

'Don't worry, I'll let you know if you're in the top four with me,' smirked Grandad Ray.

I left the house and rammed my earbuds in.

'*Hey, it's ten past eight and finally it's time to find out who the top four are in Radio Star. And what a prize there is up for grabs. My amazing show for a whole week while I'm on holiday. Hundreds of you have entered, but I have used my years of experience making fantastic radio to pick four contenders who have made it to the big grand final. Drum roll, please, Neil . . .*' said Howie. 'Neil' was Howard 'The Howie' Wright's producer and often you'd hear Howie asking him for sound effects live on air.

I walked slowly down the street. I could hardly breathe.

'*Thanks, Neil. OK, the top four are . . . a black-belt postman who serves birthday cards and the community, known simply in his entry as . . . Sensei Terry,*' announced Howie. Up ahead on the road I saw Sensei Terry almost fall off his post bike. He was obviously listening too. I loved Sensei Terry, but shouldn't he just stick to letters and karate? There were more surprises to come, though.

'*Also making the final four . . . a headmaster who wants to be a DJ – Mr Harris from St Brenda's school.*'

YOU ARE KIDDING ME, HOWIE???

Fish Face was in the final four? How? This was devastating. There were only two places left. My heart was pounding. I'd stopped walking now and had to lean against the local pet shop window. A parrot in a cage gave me a death stare.

'*And funnily enough, joining Mr Harris is one of his own pupils – it's this town's youngest DJ, Radio Boy, also known as Spike Hughes. The headmaster versus one of his pupils, now that's going to cause a bit of tension at school, right? Am I right, gang?*'

I WAS IN! I fell to the pavement and put my hands to my face; I was shaking and started to cry. Happy tears. The relief. I was in the final four.

My happy tears soon dried up.

'*The last person in the final four . . . a lovable grandad, it's the ballroom banter of Grandad Ray. The amazing thing is, radio must be in the family, as this guy is real-life grandad to Radio Boy. So, get this . . . Spike Hughes*

is going up against his grandad AND his headmaster! Wow.'

No, Howie, Grandad Ray is going up against *me*, not the other way round.

'Oh, please, no,' I shouted to no one but myself and the universe. I was a good half-mile away from home, but I swear I heard a very loud cheer from the direction of my house. Mr Harris was bad enough, but this was a nightmare of epic proportions.

Grandad Ray had made it into Howie's final four.

My grandad, my headmaster, my postman, all against me.

'So there we have our final four and I've come up with the perfect test of your broadcasting skills. The grand final is next weekend at our County Spring Fair. Each finalist will face a live on-air challenge, requiring them to interview someone at the Fair. Not as simple as it sounds, folks. How will they cope with the nerves of being live on air? Not in a cosy studio, but in the chaos of an outside broadcast at the Spring Fair. Being watched by people. Heard by millions. So close to the big prize . . . The stakes are high. The prize is huge. Come join us next week at the Spring Fair

as we find out who is THE RADIO STAR . . .'

Howie's challenge was clever. Only someone with live radio experience could survive a live link at the fair, and I was that someone. None of my rivals had much, if any, live radio experience like me. Howie had clearly chosen this as he knew it would be tailor-made for me to sail right through to victory.

I carried on my walk to school and couldn't stop thinking about Radio Star. Dreaming about winning it, on stage at the County Fair. Howie holding my hand aloft, Katherine Hamilton looking at me admiringly. Grandad Ray shaking my hand and patting me on the back.

OK, that last one was a bit far-fetched.

CHAPTER 40

The FINAL FOUR

My daydream ended as soon as I passed through the school gates.

'Well, I suppose congratulations are in order.'

As I came crashing back down to earth, I saw Mr Harris's big fishy face looming above me. Like a starving great white shark who'd spotted a nice juicy penguin in the shallows.

'Oh, thanks, Mr Harris,' I stuttered.

'Not for you, for ME!' said Mr Harris, laughing heartily

at his own non-joke. Just how had this scaly monster made the final four in my beloved Radio Star competition?

'I will be the winner, of course. Oh yes, with my years of taking assemblies, a silly interview at the Spring Fair will be no trouble for yours truly,' said Mr Harris, nodding his head in agreement with his own thoughts.

'I think you will struggle, sadly, Spike. Away from your . . . *shed* and chums, like a fish out of water. Very hard for you. As for that psycho postman . . .' Mr Harris touched the side of his face, remembering where Sensei Terry had expertly karate-kicked him. 'Well, run along now, boy,' he said, shooing me away, keen to get the memory out of his mind.

I bumped into Holly and Artie in the classroom, who greeted me with pats on the back and a hug.

'You've got a lot of work to do, Spike,' said Holly. 'We can hone your interviewing skills. I have a plan. You won't like it, but it will make you better and get you fit for the big final.'

After school, I headed home, and as I entered my road Sensei Terry found me.

'Hey, Spike, well done. Amazing news,' he said.

'Thanks, Sensei. You too, can't believe you made it. Good luck,' I said.

'I won't win, Spike. That's not my journey. That's *your* path,' said Sensei Terry mystically. He then gave me a half-bow and walked off. Humble, kind and gracious as ever. The opposite reaction was waiting for me when I got back home.

'ITTTTTTT'S THE FINAL COUNTDOOO OOOOWWWWWWWWNNNNNNNNN,' sang Grandad Ray as soon as he saw me.

'Well, didn't I do well, eh, Spike? You tried to stop me, but you cannot deny talent like mine. Ye of little faith, grandson! "Lovable" – not my words, your man Howie this morning. Sounds like he's got a favourite already,' said Grandad Ray.

'HE WAS JUST BEING KIND,' I spat out. Grandad drove me mad. Hair-gelled grandad from hell. Stealer of grandkids' dreams.

'Hey, take it easy, Radio Boy. Don't get rattled,' he said.

'I AM NOT,' I yelled. Proving him right. I calmed myself. Then spoke.

'So how's Nan, Grandad? Spoken to her lately?' I said. I wasn't going down so easily.

His big smug grin turned upside down at that.

'I . . . I . . . erm . . . not sure. OK, I think,' he said.

I suddenly felt a bit bad. Crushing your grandad doesn't feel very good.

'Well, you'll see her next weekend as she loves the Spring Fair, doesn't she?' I asked.

'Yes, she does,' Grandad Ray mumbled quietly. He'd got to me and I had really got to him. Then Mum came flying in at her usual rate of two hundred miles an hour. Still dressed in her hospital uniform.

'Well, congratulations to you both! How lovely! You're both in the final,' she said.

Lovely? Not really. I headed up to my bedroom, more worried than excited. Was Grandad Ray right, did Howie have a favourite? To him, Grandad Ray was a colourful, cuddly old grandad. The kind talent shows love. The thought of him winning was unbearable.

A voice came from downstairs.

'Hey, Spike, your dad's on the teatime news! Come watch, they're live at his supermarket.'

Why can't my family just be normal?

CHAPTER 41

Training camp

The few days leading up to Dad's *Search For a Star* semi-finals were spent brushing up on my interviewing skills. My training was designed by Coach Holly and her loyal assistant, Artie. One hideously embarrassing training exercise invented by Holly was 'Operation Park Bench'. I'm sure she came up with it just to see me glow so bright red with embarrassment, you could've spotted me from the International Space Station.

I was under strict Holly orders to sit for two hours on a park bench and interview anyone – I repeat, anyone – who came and sat down on the bench next to me. How do you start chatting to random strangers? From their point of view, they go to the park to eat their cheese-and-pickle sandwich in the fresh outdoors and this random kid who's sat there starts asking them their life story.

'Hi, I'm Spike.'

SILENCE. Munch. Munch.

'Yes . . . um . . . I'm training for a radio competition by interviewing people – can I interview you?'

SILENCE. Munch munch (a little faster, like they're trying to finish up quickly). Then they get out their packet of crisps.

'It won't take very long.'

THEY STARE AT ME FOR THIRTY LONG SECONDS. CRUNCH.

I smile pleadingly.

THEY WALK OFF.

Not everyone did that, though; a few stayed on the bench and chatted to me. At first I was a mumbling, sweating mess, but after each one Holly would listen back to the recording of the interview, making notes. Assistant interview trainer Artie would always appear from a bush from where he had been recording the chat and offer the tolerant stranger a cake from his dad's cake shop (Mr Cake) by way of thanks.

Chief training officer Holly was brutal with her interview feedback. I don't think anyone had ever explained the concept of gentle constructive criticism to her.

'That was shocking, Spike! What's this awful strange new laugh you've started doing?' she asked me, handing me her headphones so I could hear the full horror.

Me to Stranger: 'You here to feed the ducks? Huh huh huh he he he.'

She was right, I barely recognised the hideous laugh, but it was mine.

Holly frowned. 'Spike, just stop trying so hard, just relax and be you.'

'I know, but I feel so awkward and boring,' I said.

'You can do better. Let's go again – quick, Artie, back in the bushes, there's an old lady about to sit on the bench,' said Holly as she motioned at the tiny old lady walking slowly towards me.

The old lady eventually got to my bench and slowly sat down after wiping it with her gloved hand. I gave her my usual unsuccessful interview request, telling her about the Radio Star competition and how I was practising my skills. Only she didn't walk off like most of the others; she smiled, sat down next to me, and her blue eyes twinkled.

'I'd love to chat to you, young man. I don't talk to anyone much these days, since my poor husband died,' she said.

'Oh, I'm sorry to hear that. What was his name?'

'Geoff. He loved this park.'

'When did he . . . um . . . pass?' I asked.

'A few months ago,' she sighed. I felt really sorry for her.

'How long had you been married?'

'Over sixty years.'

'Amazing. You must really miss him.'

'I do. I talk to him every day still, though,' she said.

Oh, poor lady. She was obviously a little bit mad. This happens, I think, to old people. Artie's grandad is in something called a 'home' after his wife died. This seems to be like a prison for old people who haven't really committed any crime, apart from getting old.

'How nice to be able to have a chat with you,' I said. I did my best 'it's OK, old crazy lady' smile.

'Oh, I know what you're thinking – you reckon I'm mad,' she said and winked.

'Not at all,' I said. Lying bare-faced.

'I come here to this bench and chat to my Geoff in my head, and in my heart,' she said, smiling and looking up at the sun.

She held her head back and smiled even more. As if she was soaking in the rays. A tiny little tear rolled slowly down her cheek. Then I noticed one was rolling down mine too. I tried quickly to dry my eyes, but she saw me.

'It's OK to cry, Spike – shows you have a big heart.' She patted me on the arm.

'You must be . . . um . . . lonely,' I said.

'Yes,' she replied simply. 'I have my son, but he's busy – well, you young people always are. But I don't get to speak to people that much.'

I glanced over to where two dog walkers had just bumped into each other and were chatting, introducing their dogs. That was a thing about having a dog. You always end up talking to other dog owners. The dogs themselves don't really say much to each other, just sniff each other's bums and look bored.

'You should get a dog,' I said. 'That way you'd meet people every time you walked it in the park.'

She smiled. 'That's not a bad idea, actually. My son is a dog trainer, as it happens.'

I smiled back, my eyes still a bit teary. 'Why do you come here, to *this* bench?' I said, trying to pull myself together.

'Because Geoff and I have been coming to eat our sandwiches on this bench for over forty years – it's our bench,' she said.

I stifled down more tears. I wondered how many times they'd sat here. I got even sadder when I feared Katherine Hamilton and I may never get to have 'our' bench. Then an idea came to me, and this time it was a good one.

'We should *really* make it your bench,' I said excitedly.

'How?' she asked.

'With this.' I showed her my front door key.

'And then what?' she asked, still not catching on.

'You carve it into the wood,' I said. 'Mark it as yours.'

'I've never graffitied in my life, young man!'

'Well, you're never too old to start,' I said. She gave me a sly grin and her eyes twinkled again. And so I helped an old lady carve her and her husband's name into a park bench:

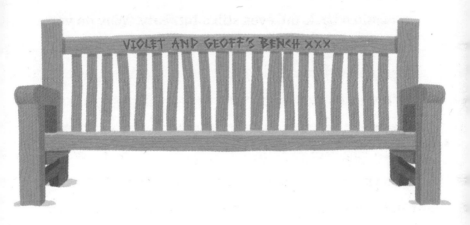

She stood up and looked back at her work.

'He's laughing,' she said quietly. I bet he was. 'Well, I'll leave you now,' she added.

'No, I'll leave you to have a chat with Geoff. It's your bench, after all. Thanks for talking to me, Violet.' I stood up.

'My pleasure. Thank you for talking to me, and good luck in your competition,' she said.

I thanked her, began walking away, and saw Holly and Artie coming out from the bushes. As I looked back at my new friend Violet, I made a note to myself. Never again, when I saw someone old, would I just look through them. I would try to think of who they are and wonder what story they might have.

Just as I had this very important thought, I saw a furious-looking park warden marching towards Violet and the freshly graffitied park bench. But sometimes in life, magic happens. Just as I was fearing Violet might get arrested and be put in a 'home', a football came flying over with supernatural force from the nearby pitch.

With absolute precision, it hit the park warden with just enough power to ensure he stumbled and fell head-first into the duck pond. Allowing my new friend Violet to walk on, hassle-free.

I looked over to the football pitch to where the ball had come from. Not only could I not see the kicker, the football pitch was completely empty.

Maybe it was the ghost of old Geoff.

Three days until the winner of Radio Star is found.

Me?

Mr Harris?

Sensei Terry?

Or – please no – Grandad Ray.

CHAPTER 42

ATTACK of the DADS

Nothing can prepare you in life for the unexpected sight of your mum putting make-up on your own dad's face to make him look like a pirate. I repeat. A PIRATE.

Today was the *Search For a Star* semi-final. As Mum was 'pirating-up' my dad, my sister and I set to work on our home-made banner. A supportive gesture for our beloved father. Or more accurately, just doing what Mum had ordered us to do.

Mum: 'Why don't you two make your dad a banner to cheer him on?'

Us: 'No thanks.'

Mum: 'YOU WILL or no TV for a year.'

All Mum's threats were completely OTT and involved this formula:

<u>something we enjoy</u> x <u>banned for a ridiculous length of time</u> = MumThreat

i.e.,

No daylight for one month

No sleep for three months

No water for six months

She ran our home like a maximum-security prison at times.

Top similarities between a prison and my house:

1. Random searches at any time. ('What's in your pockets? Empty them RIGHT NOW!')
2. Lights out at 8pm.

3. Zero chance of escape.
4. Scary cell-mate (Grandad Ray).

Soon it was time to say goodbye to Dad as he left once more for the TV studios. We would be seeing him later, as we were allowed to be in the audience.

The horror show started earlier than I thought when Mum told Amber and me to go and get ready. I remained sitting on the couch, because I would be going in what I was wearing. My trademark outfit of T-shirt and jeans. However, I was hugely mistaken, apparently.

'Oh no, young man. No son of mine is appearing on national television dressed like he's hanging around the shopping precinct. Go and put your school uniform on.'

'WHAT?'

'I've washed it.'

'No way, Mum, come on! You can't be serious?' I protested.

'You will look cute and a real Mr Smarty Pants.'

'Please, Mum, no, it's embarrassing,' I said.

'GET CHANGED NOW OR NO RADIO SHOW FOR

THE REST OF THE YEAR,' said the prison warden.

Despite the unrealistic threat, it was pointless arguing. I dragged myself upstairs to my bedroom and slammed the door.

I put my uniform on, and took a look at myself in the mirror. I hated what I saw. I opened my bedroom door and Grandad Ray was standing on the landing.

'Oh wow, you're going in fancy dress,' he said as he combed back his glistening nest of hair. He was positively reeking of his signature scent. *L'Homme Odour Toilet.*

'*You're* coming?' I asked.

'Wouldn't miss it for the world, see my son make a fool of himself again,' he said, putting his comb in his back pocket. It was in that moment I decided that I would be The Pirates' biggest fan. Just to show I wasn't like Grandad Ray.

I'd never been to a TV studio before. It was like an aircraft hangar, with people walking around very quickly, carrying clipboards and wearing headsets. We skipped the large queue of audience members when a clipboard headset lady came to meet us.

'Hi, I'm Vogue,' she said. Was that even a name? It

sounded like a make of car. *The Ford Vogue.*

Vogue led us smartly through a labyrinth of corridors; cables were everywhere. Cables bigger and thicker than I'd ever seen before. As Vogue slowed down, we saw a giant sign: 'SILENCE, LIVE TRANSMISSION IN PROGRESS'.

I gulped. On the wall above the sign was written in big red letters, STUDIO 1. Underneath was a white wipeboard that had '**SFAS**' on it. We were at the actual recording studio. Vogue pushed back the biggest curtain I had ever seen. It went up and up and up, and then Mum, Amber, Grandad Ray and I went inside.

The first thing that hit me was how cold it was. Then all the lights, hundreds of them. Finally I saw them. The TV cameras. So many of them, at least four and one on a crane. Even Grandad Ray's eyes were popping out. It was unbelievable.

The stage was big, but not as big as it seemed on TV. We walked past the judges' desk – a new one after Dad had broken the last one. I saw the four judges' chairs. We were shown to our seats, which were marked RESERVED: GUESTS. I was so excited. One day my life would involve all this.

'Have you just come straight from school?' asked Vogue, looking at me and seeming a bit confused as it was Saturday night.

'Oh no! He just wanted to look smart on TV,' lied my mum.

We took our seats and then more guests were ushered in, the families of other finalists. They looked at us and us back at them like the rivals we were. I was the only one in school uniform. I must've looked like I'd been allowed out of my posh private boarding school for the weekend.

The rest of the audience poured in excitedly. The place was now buzzing. At the back of the stage on a screen that was the size of a football pitch, a countdown clock appeared.

17 : 29 : 13

Not long now until we were live to the whole country. I was getting butterflies and I wasn't even performing. Goodness knows how my dad was coping.

A man in a shiny suit came out and Mum told us this was a 'warm-up man'. As his job title suggested, his job was to 'warm' us all up. Loud music started playing and my mum immediately demonstrated that she didn't need any warming up, by whooping at the top of her voice. Everyone looked over to see who the crazy woman was; *Hey, everyone, meet my mum.*

The warm-up man told us what was going to happen tonight and then introduced the judges. First what appeared to be someone's nan walked out, called Sheila, I think, who was married to a very old rock star. Then someone else who was a record producer, and then a young woman who'd had one hit that my sister played all the time called 'Booty Booty'. Then finally the man we were all here to see: Simon Scowl. Out he sauntered in pointy high boots, his shirt as always halfway undone and the worst haircut on TV. He waved at us like the Queen does. Like, 'Yes yes whatever'. The warm-up man handed Simon the microphone. He was smaller than on TV.

'Hi, everyone,' he said, and the place went crazy. Screaming and foot stamping.

'Thanks for coming, enjoy all the acts, have a great night.' And he sat down on his purple-cushioned throne. The countdown clock showed **4: 23: 19** until showtime. I was so nervous. Mum leaned into me. 'He'll be fine, don't worry.'

Grandad Ray muttered, 'I hope he's taken those tummy tablets.'

The clock hit zero as the theme tune started playing.

The first act was introduced. 'Juggling is hard – juggling on a unicycle is really hard – JUGGLING CHAINSAWS ON A UNICYCLE IS IMPOSSIBLE, or is it?' said the very enthusiastic hosts in tight trousers.

A wide-eyed madman cycled out on to the stage on a unicycle. He hopped off and started up three chainsaws. In case we had any doubt as to whether they were real (who makes fake chainsaws?), the mad unicyclist chopped through some pieces of wood. An equally mad-looking assistant came out and as the wide-eyed madman got back on to his unicycle, the assistant handed him the first chainsaw. Then another. Then the juggling started. He juggled the chainsaws as if they were apples. The crowd were gasping and clapping. Everyone was transfixed as the third chainsaw was added. Mum had her hands over her mouth in shock.

The hosts came back out and then stared down the TV camera, with their serious faces, urging any children watching 'not to try this at home'. Gee, thanks. First of all, we don't have a single chainsaw, let alone three of them, and, secondly, it's not as if I'm getting bored of having arms and fancied a change by losing them juggling chainsaws.

After the essential chainsaw safety talk, the hosts shouted some more words that were hard to make out over the noise of the audience, but I did pick out all too clearly the words 'The Pirates' and 'Up next'.

I felt myself sinking deeper into my seat.

As the rest of the country was putting the kettle on or going to the toilet during the ad break, we saw them getting the stage ready for Dad's band. The mic stand for Tom the lead singer, Dad's drums and the band's amps. Fake rigging was slowly lowered from the ceiling by the stage hands and various props were added to make the stage look like a pirate ship.

And suddenly we were back live and the excitable hosts did their introduction.

'Now, this band went viral in their audition when their drummer not only knocked out a cameraman, but stage-dived on to Simon's desk . . .' Cue hysterical laughter from the judges. I was now bouncing up and down, Mum was almost out of her seat with excitement, Grandad Ray was asleep. GRANDAD RAY WAS ASLEEP!

And snoring very loudly.

I shook him awake. 'What? Where am I? Did the tiger eat my hair?' He had drooled down his chin.

'You fell asleep in here? With all this noise?' I said.

'I was just resting my eyes.'

'Here they are now,' I said, pointing as the lights went up on the stage, revealing the band dressed as even silkier pirates than last time, and standing on their own wooden pirate boat.

This was it.

I took a deep breath.

CHAPTER 43

Zombie Mum

My dad started a loud drum roll. Tom, the lead pirate, started to speak from the steering wheel of the fake wooden boat. Dad corrected me later, telling me that it was not a steering wheel, but *the helm*. As if he was now a nautical expert, having sat drumming in a fake wooden boat in a TV studio!

'Let me introduce the band,' Tom announced. 'On bass we have Driftwood Dave . . .' Cue audience applause. *Driftwood Dave?* Driftwood Dave is an insurance salesman. Dad said they had a few new ideas and surprises for tonight's show – giving the band members pirate-themed names was obviously one of them.

'On the drums, it's Captain Scurvy.' *Captain Scurvy.* This was my dad! The audience whooped and cheered as the infamous drummer was introduced.

'And I'm Shark Tooth Tom,' said Tom Dribble, tanning salon king. 'This song's called "Walk the Plank of My Love".'

And with that Dad did his drumstick thing and actually caught them this time. The song was about a one-toothed lady pirate with scurvy. Scurvy is the disease pirates and sailors got from not eating enough fruit. The chorus went:

'*You only got one tooth, but you got my heart,*
Rickety lady,
Come walk the plank of my love.'

The Pirates' performance ended with Dad's drum kit exploding. Weirdly, nothing went horribly wrong.

The audience cheered wildly and Simon Scowl stood up and clapped them. I have to admit I clapped too. I even whooped at one point.

The lighthouse search beam sought us out in row G and found Grandad Ray with a face like thunder. He was so jealous at Dad getting so much audience love.

'Grown men behaving like that – Captain Scurvy, how embarrassing,' he mumbled, almost drowned out by the cheering as The Pirates left the stage.

Dad was scanning the crowd, looking for us.

'DAD!' I yelled. He stopped, squinted into the crowd and his eyes lit up when he found us all waving.

He waved back with his drumsticks, grinning.

Mum was also on her feet, waving at him frantically. She was crying.

'What's up?' I asked her.

'I'm just so proud of him. He looked so happy up there,' she said as she looked round to smile at me, and I almost screamed at the sight of her face. The tears had made her make-up run, so she looked like a horror-movie zombie.

The other acts came and went, and it became very clear that the audience had one big favourite. It was another lady with a dog that barked like it was singing to various songs. It was pretty cool. I wondered if Sherlock could be trained to do this, as there seemed to be a big market for performing dogs. I quickly started forming a shortlist of things I could try to teach Sherlock:

1. Roller-skating
2. Trampolining
3. Water-skiing

All the acts came back on stage to hear the results and who was going into the big final.

After lots of dramatic pauses and drum rolls, it turned out Pawboy the singing poodle from South Wales had sunk The Pirates.

It was over. Dad's band were out.

But, strangely, it didn't feel sad, and Dad didn't look sad when we met him at the stage door later.

'It was all about the fun,' he said. 'And that *was* fun, right?'

'Yeah,' I admitted.

He was right. It *had* been fun. Even if I was still in my school uniform.

'Bit rubbish, though,' said Grandad. 'The barking dog was much better.'

Dad caught my eye and winked at me. I winked back.

1 DAY UNTIL THE RADIO STAR GRAND FINAL. ME VS THE WORLD.

CHAPTER 44

You said WHAT?

I woke up the next morning to find my sister looming over me, her face far too close to mine for comfort.

'Wake up, you idiot, Spike, you're missing all this! Dad and The Pirates have been offered a record deal!'

We ran downstairs silently (which is quite a skill), positioning ourselves on the spy step on the stairs. A record deal? Wow, Dad was going to be mega-famous. How would this affect me? A bigger house: hopefully a mansion like Artie's, with its own driveway. Holidays in foreign countries. Luxury loo rolls, not like that cheap stuff Dad brings home from his supermarket. A bigger TV. NEW SHED!

I was about to leap into the kitchen from the stairs when Amber grabbed me and shot me a warning glance. Inside, Grandad Ray and Dad were shouting at each other in whispers.

I didn't like what I was not supposed to be hearing.

'You said *no* to the record deal?' said Grandad Ray incredulously. I was incredulous too, and I'm not even sure I know what that word means. Good name for a rapper, though.

'Yes, it's not for me,' Dad said. How was he being so calm when he'd just said no to a bigger house, luxury world cruises and endless supplies of luxurious toilet roll?

'Simon Scowl offers you a record contract and big UK tour and you say NO? I'd have given anything for a chance like that, anything,' said Grandad Ray.

'I'm not you, though. I won't give up everything. Especially not my family. *Then* I'd be you,' said Dad.

Ouch.

'I had talent and a dream – some people don't understand that,' said Grandad.

'My dream is of having a family I love and who love me, that's what makes me happy. I'd ruin that by saying yes to Simon Scowl and spending half my life away on the road. It's been fun being in the band again, but that was enough.'

'You're making a huge mistake, one you'll regret for the rest of your life, standing counting packets of biscuits in that dreary supermarket,' said Grandad Ray.

Low punch.

'I'd rather be stacking biscuits than lose what I have with Carol and my kids,' said Dad.

My heart swelled when he said that. *He really loves us. Even though he buys us cheap loo roll.* My sister lost interest at this point and went back to her room to apply her kilo of make-up and get on the phone for the next seventeen hours to a boy called Ralph who was definitely *not* her boyfriend, according to her. Except he was. But when this was suggested by any of us, she would shout *'He is not!'* so loudly you could hear her several postcodes away.

Dad walked out and spotted me before I could disappear too.

'What are you doing, Spike?' he said.

'Listening to you and Grandad arguing. I can't believe you turned down a record deal,' I said.

'Come with me,' he said, and we headed out into the garden. He walked to the shed and went inside.

'Sit down,' Dad said. 'I know this will be hard for you to understand at your age, but me trying to chase fame, thinking it would make me happier, would be a mistake. I'd be away from you guys too much. That's what—'

'I know,' I said. 'I heard you telling Grandad. But . . . your job is sooo boring.' It came out meaner than I meant.

'It's not that bad. I know all the customers' names. I know old Mrs Williams can never find the puddings. That Mr Hamilton buys chocolate eclairs and eats them in his car so his wife doesn't tell him off. I like chatting to them. I like my family. I like my life. I'm happy. You know who *isn't* happy?'

'Who?'

'Grandad,' said Dad. 'He's not a bad man, Spike, but I grew up with a dad who cared more about trying to get famous than his family. It made him unhappy in the end, and now even Nan has had enough. I promised myself that if I became a dad I wouldn't do that, and I would remember what's really important in life. That's why I said no to Simon Scowl.'

In that moment I realised my dad was my hero.

'Choices,' I said.

'Choices, yeah,' said Dad, drifting off. I caught his eyes as he stared out of the shed window, which wasn't that easy due to the cobwebs. He looked miles away. Maybe on a wooden pirate boat on a stage he wouldn't be getting on now. I guess some choices aren't easy.

CHAPTER 45

Friends reunited

So the day of the big final for me was here at last. Today was the County Spring Fair. The winner of Radio Star would be crowned there. I was more nervous than I'd ever been.

The County Spring Fair was held annually just out of town in a huge park. There were hundreds of stalls selling various things you don't normally see in the high street. Maybe for good reason. Lots of things made out of shells, home-made candles, fudge the size of rocks, and lots of men in leather waistcoats making things from wood. There were also tents filled with livestock, horses with their best hairdos and a huge arena for shows that ran all day. Not forgetting giant marquees filled with cakes, oversized vegetables on steroids, cheeses, and the rest of the men in leather waistcoats drinking home-made beer that looked like mud. Easter-egg hunts for kids and the usual face painters.

As me, Mum and Dad arrived, Dad got spotted and asked for his autograph by an old lady carrying an enormous fruit cake that had a winning red rosette stuck to it. Grandad Ray strode in with his *Ballroom Banter* ladies in tow. Now the trio was down to just a duo, as the husband of the third ballroom lady was the man who'd had the 'misunderstanding' with Grandad Ray.

A loudspeaker crackled into life.

'Hi, folks, this is Howard "The Howie" Wright from Kool FM, and we are live today from the County Spring Fair; come and say hello. We are just next to the "Guess How Many Sweets are in the Jar" stall. In the next hour the grand final of Radio Star will begin. Four lucky finalists competing to be me for a week.

Right now, the falconry display is about to start in the main show arena. Watch the Flying Falcons stunt display team re-enact the Battle of Britain!'

'Good luck, Spike,' said a voice behind me. I turned to see Sensei Terry.

'Hi, Sensei, how come you're in your outfit?' I asked.

'*Gi*, Spike, *gi*. I'm doing a karate demonstration later,' he said as his eyes scanned the crowds, as if half expecting to be suddenly attacked by a crazed sword-wielding ninja.

'What do you do?' I asked.

'Break bricks,' he replied matter-of-factly. As if nothing he had just said was out of the ordinary.

'What?' I asked.

'My hands are like sharpened axes; tools. I focus my *chi* through them.'

I looked at him as if he was mad. How can a human break a brick with his hands? As I made my way through the slow-moving crowd, I bumped into Holly. She was with Artie and we saw a coconut shy. This is the stand where you try to throw small balls at coconuts on stands to knock them off.

We headed over. 'I haven't got too long,' I said.

As we approached, I saw that Martin Harris and Katherine Hamilton were about to have a go. They clocked us, looked at Holly and sniggered.

'Oh, you OK now, Holly? Not going to get scared again, are you?' said Katherine in a very sarcastic way.

Holly walked past them and paid for three balls.

'I bet I do better than you,' she challenged Martin.

Oh, Holly, I thought, *why did you do that? The ape boy is a sporting genetic freak. Captain of the school football, rugby and cricket teams. He will thrash you.*

'You sure you want to do this?' I whispered.

She ignored me, her eyes staring right through Martin.

'Really, you think you can beat *me*?' he said. 'It would be embarrassing for you, and you've already embarrassed yourself enough recently,' he sneered.

Holly didn't rise to him; she just calmly said, 'You can go first.'

'Fine. Let's do it, three balls each.' Martin eyed the coconuts, picked one to be his first target and fixed his mutant eye on it, took aim, then launched with tremendous power. His ball smashed into the coconut on the far right, knocking it off its stand and to the ground. Katherine Hamilton cheered and clapped like a demented sea lion. I felt like throwing up at the sight of her sickening display of affection.

Holly took aim and threw her ball. Then her second, then her third, with blinding speed. One, two, three coconuts clattered to the ground, almost simultaneously. The old man running the stall yelled, 'WOW! I've never seen anything like that in my twenty years of running this stall. Have your money back, young lady.'

Martin gulped. Trying his best not to be impressed and hiding the fact all the pressure was on him now. 'Lucky shots,' he mumbled.

He took aim again, taking longer this time to make sure he was ready. He launched and . . . THUD. His ball hit the back of the tent, missing the coconut.

Katherine Hamilton touched his shoulder and said, 'Maybe you threw it too hard.'

'Be quiet,' Martin hissed angrily.

He took aim again, took even longer this time. Artie sneezed and Martin spun round, glaring at him.

'Sorry – hay fever,' said Artie.

Martin settled himself again. He had to hit this one.

'Good luck,' offered Holly.

Martin snarled. He took aim and threw with all his might. It missed by miles. The old man running the stall gave him a slow handclap and chuckled. 'I think the young lady just beat you.'

'Who cares? Stupid game. You just got lucky,' burst out a very red-faced Martin Harris.

'I'm sure you're right,' agreed Holly. She then picked up three more balls. Closed her eyes and did the same trick again. Fired off three shots one after the other. Knocking down the two Martin hadn't been able to, and one more for luck. A small crowd had gathered, waiting to play, and burst into applause.

'Awesome!' a little boy said, taking a break from licking his ice cream to appreciate Holly's party trick. Katherine Hamilton stood transfixed on the spot. 'Cool,' she said.

Martin stormed off through the crowd.

'How on earth did you do that?' I asked.

'Faith, trusting my instincts. Just like you need to do today,' Holly said and smiled at me.

I said goodbye to Artie and Holly and made my way to where I'd been instructed to go by Kool FM in the letter they'd sent me. The letter congratulated me on making it to the final of Radio Star and I'd been about to get it framed until I saw it was addressed to a 'Mr Pike Huge'. My handwriting wasn't the neatest, I'll admit, but how could anyone send that letter, thinking there was someone called 'Pike Huge'?

I saw their radio station broadcast truck with a big antenna on top. I said hello to a lady with a clipboard.

'Yes! Radio Boy, is it? Pike Huge,' she said and looked at her list.

'Yes but no,' I said.

'Sorry?' she said.

'I am Radio Boy, but it's Spike HUGHES,' I said clearly.

'Right, sorry. There is another contestant already here – Mr Harris. He insisted we just call him that, Mr Harris. Quite an odd one, but anyway he's in our backstage area tucking into a sausage roll if you want to chill out with him. We need you in about ten minutes' time.'

'NO,' I said, a little too quickly. 'I'll take a wander and be back here in ten minutes.'

The Spring Fair was well under way. There were crying kids clutching chocolate Easter eggs the size of their heads, knackered-looking cows attached to ropes being led by farmers to show tents, and vegetable growers with prize-winning cucumbers that looked like lethal weapons in their arms. In no time at all it was time for me to head back to the Kool FM tent.

I arrived at the same moment as Grandad Ray, who was wearing a leather waistcoat. He was arm in arm with one of the *Ballroom Banter* ladies. Susan, Jackie or Daphne.

'This is Spike. Spike, this is Candice.' So: a new one.

'What happened to Susan and Daphne?' I asked, just to annoy him.

'Er, creative differences,' he said as he walked ahead quickly. We were ushered into a backstage area, which was actually a few hay bales made into scratchy seats. Fish Face was sitting bolt upright and looking very tense on one of them. His terrifying mum was stood behind him, massaging his shoulders. She smiled at me in a sinister way. Like a crocodile might do when inviting you to lunch. I looked away, before she could steal my soul, and found Sensei Terry was sitting cross-legged on the floor with his eyes closed, meditating.

Grandad Ray muttered something I couldn't hear under his breath when he spotted Sensei Terry. Sensei Terry, without even opening an eye, said quietly, 'The coward whispers, the wise man says nothing.'

'Whatever,' said Grandad Ray.

Howard 'The Howie' Wright came powering into the backstage/hay-bale area wearing a very bright Hawaiian shirt and Crocs. It was devastating to see my hero in plastic shoes with air vents. I could only hope and pray his actual shoes had been pooped on by some of the animals, and the Crocs were an emergency replacement.

'HEY HEY! Is that *fear* I smell or is it llama poop?' The Howie laughed very loudly at this joke. 'Welcome, everyone,' he said. He looked at all of us.

'Obviously you're the headmaster, Mr Harris,' he said, offering his hand to Fish Face to shake.

'Yes! What gave it away?' boomed Fish Face.

'You're the only person here in a suit and tie, classic headmaster outfit,' joked Howard 'The Howie'

Wright, looking at everyone, expecting laughter. We gave it nervously. Apart from Fish Face himself, of course.

'If you're referring to my being smartly attired, as befits my standing in the community, then good. I am a headmaster and cannot be seen looking scruffy by my pupils or their parents.' Maybe it was my imagination, but I thought Howard 'The Howie' Wright looked a little bit scared.

'Y-y-yes, of course,' spluttered Howard 'The Howie' Wright, and moved away. 'You are Sensei Terry.' Easy guess, given the karate *gi*.

'Nice to meet you, Howard,' said Sensei Terry as he shook The Howie's hand and gave him a half-bow.

The presenter's eyes now took in Grandad Ray.

'Wow,' was all he could say. His eyes had only made it as far as Grandad Ray's hair.

The best was yet to come.

Grandad Ray spread his legs and started to murder another song at the top of his voice. It came to a dramatic end when he went down on one knee, offering his hand to Howie and bellowing, 'I'm your man!'

'Amazing!' said Howard, clapping enthusiastically. Neil, his producer, did the same. I got the feeling his producer was like his butler.

Holly isn't like that to me. She's too smart for that. I'm more like *her* butler.

'You're a real star, Ray, and I love *Ballroom Banter*,' said Howard 'The Howie' Wright. My blood turned icy cold as I saw that Grandad Ray was clearly The Howie's favourite.

'Radio Boy, Spike. Great to see you again. You remind me of what I was like at your age,' he turned to me and said, lifting my spirits sky high. He must mean my undeniable raw exciting talent.

'My mum dressed me as well,' he joked, referring to the leaping dolphin jumper I was wearing. Mum had made me, saying it was cute. At least it wasn't a leather waistcoat.

'OK, all of you. Good luck. Neil will explain what's going to happen; I'll see you on the other side,' said Howard 'The Howie' Wright.

Neil the producer told us the rules. Each one of us would have to interview someone here at the Spring Fair – someone chosen by them. In each case it would be a person who had won a prize here. Mr Harris was told he would be first and interviewing the person who had won Best County Fair Baker.

'I love cake!' said Mr Harris.

'Great news, that should help you – come with me,' said Neil the producer.

Grandad Ray, Sensei Terry and I stayed backstage on the hay bales. We could hear everything from the speakers. Holly and Artie turned up to keep me company and wish me luck.

'You look petrified, Spike,' Holly said, concerned.

'Yeah, I think The Howie, my radio hero, wants Grandad Ray to win,' I said.

'Look, Spike, you are great at listening to people and talking to them on the radio. That's your superpower. It's just a silly talent competition anyway,' Holly said.

It didn't seem silly to me. It was my ticket out of the garden shed and on to radio stardom.

'*Now on Kool FM, it's the first of the four Radio Star finalists, the headmaster from St Brenda's, Mr Harris, who is live at the cake tent . . .*' said the backstage speaker.

Howie introduced Mr Harris and we all stopped talking.

'. . . Hello, am I live? Is this thing on . . .' was all we heard from Mr Harris. A reassuringly rubbish start.

'Right, hello, County Fair. This is Mr Harris from Merit Radio, the school radio station of St Brenda's, the best education establishment around! I am here with . . .' What a surprise – Fish Face had forgotten the name of the person he was supposed to be interviewing.

'Glenn Tims!' said Fish Face loudly into the microphone. I'm guessing Neil the producer had already told him five times. 'Yes, Glenn Tims, who has just won best baker – well done, Glenn.'

'Thanks, I'm very happy.' But Glenn Tims didn't sound like it.

'Tell us about this amazing-looking cake,' said Fish Face.

'Well, it's three levels. The first is a salted chocolate caramel base,' said Glenn Tims in a croaky voice. Something wasn't right.

'A stunning cake. Have you been baking long?' asked Fish Face.

'Since I was a child. Don't you remember me, Mr

Harris?' asked Glenn Tims aggressively.

If the rest of the County Fair was anything like the backstage hay-bales area, all ears were suddenly on what was going out on Kool FM right now. No one was talking and our eyes were suddenly glued to the little TV monitor recording the interviews for Kool FM's website.

'Do I . . . know you?' Fish Face asked, slowly and nervously. One thing was for sure, this was unmissable radio.

'I went to St Brenda's, Mr Harris,' said Glenn Tims.

'Really? Was I there back then?' asked Fish Face tentatively.

'Oh yes, Mr Harris, and you made my life hell,' said Glenn Tims. Right now I imagined even the rare-breed sheep had stopped munching the grass to hear this out.

'Oh . . . I'm sure it wasn't that bad. School can be tough for some, but here you are now with this amazing cake—'

'You made MY LIFE HELL! Told me only girls bake cakes, in front of the whole class,' said Glenn Tims, who was starting to weep into the checked tea towel over his shoulder.

Silence. Silence from the cake tent. All that was barely audible was the heavy breathing of Mr Harris. I think I heard him gulp.

'I never would've said that. You must have me confused with another teacher, perhaps Mrs Warble, the home economics teacher? Dragon of a lady, very precious about Bakewell tarts, I recall. It was years ago, memories get distorted.'

'Mrs Warble taught me all I know about a good rise on a Victoria sponge. How dare you speak ill of her! It was you – how could anyone forget your stinking coffee breath,' said Glenn Tims. The weeping had stopped and it now seemed as if Glenn was a bubbling volcano about to erupt.

'How insulting! Well, maybe I saw something in you back then that I'm seeing now – your rudeness!'

And that was all it took for Glenn Tims's volcano of school misery to explode.

Years of nightmares about a cruel headmaster, and the crushing of a young boy's dreams of becoming a pastry chef, all came boiling to the surface. Suddenly Mr Glenn Tims was presented with a chance to gain his revenge, and the only weapon at his immediate disposal was a giant salted-caramel cake of prize-winning standard. With barely a moment's hesitation, Glenn lifted his precious cake into the air and rocket-propelled it into Mr Harris's very surprised and fishy face.

CHAPTER 46

The 'AMAZING' tent

After Glenn Tims had unleashed years of anger at his old tormentor, Mr Harris, with a salted-caramel cake bomb, he was dragged away kicking and screaming to the show security tent.

No one had any sympathy for Mr Harris, though – everyone just felt sorry for poor Glenn Tims. Safe to say, Fish Face's bid to win Radio Star was not looking good.

Backstage, Sensei Terry shared some ancient wisdom. 'Anger is like holding on to a hot coal, expecting the other person to get burned. You are the person who gets burned.'

'Holding on to hot coal? What are you talking about, Kung Fu Terry?' sneered Grandad Ray.

'Not my words. Ancient Buddhist saying,' said Sensei Terry.

'But I bet Glenn Tims feels better now he's finally had his revenge on that bully Fish Face,' I said.

'Cake karma,' Sensei Terry replied.

'OK, Mr Terry, you're up next,' said a rather stressed-looking Producer Neil.

'SENSEI TERRY,' said the karate-loving postman, so forcibly the power of his words almost knocked Producer Neil right off his feet.

'S-s-s-s-sorry, *Sensei* Terry,' Neil said, and correctly. 'You are interviewing the winner of the biggest cucumber competition,' he continued. 'If it's all right with you, that is, Sensei, sir.'

'Please, lead on,' encouraged Sensei Terry. I followed him out as I was keen to see how he got on.

We made our way through the crowds of people dragging fat dogs and grizzling children, slowly looking at the various stalls of goods they would later regret buying. Who really needs a sheepskin rug you make yourself at home with glue and a bag of wool, or a wood carving of a badger reading a book?

We came to a large tent with a sign boasting that it contained 'Amazing Vegetables'. That was a bit much. Who is ever 'amazed' at a vegetable? No one has ever picked up a carrot and gone, 'That carrot is truly amazing,' unless, of course, the carrot is singing the national anthem.

Straight away I was struck by the serious lack of amazing vegetables. Then I saw it. The winning cucumber. This one looked like it had been pumped full of air and was about to explode. It actually was amazing.

Producer Neil moved closer to Sensei Terry. 'Sensei Terry, this is who you will be interviewing. Margaret Babble, Winner of Most Amazing County Fair Vegetable.'

Margaret was a twinkly-eyed lady who looked like a friendly grandmother. She had big hair in a giant bun on the top of her head and could have also won an amazing hair-bun competition. She had a glass of wine in her hand. A large one, and there were a few empty glasses on her table.

Sensei Terry bowed and Margaret made 'ohhh' noises. I think this meant she was impressed.

Sensei Terry was handed a microphone and given a ten-second countdown. A crowd was gathering round him and Margaret.

'Five . . . four . . . three . . . two . . .' counted Producer Neil.

The speakers in the tent boomed once more with the sound of Howard 'The Howie' Wright live on Kool FM and around the County Fair.

'Now it's time for our second contender. Hopefully this will be . . . smoother than our earlier one. Now I go live to the vegetable tent and our karate-teaching postman, Sensei Terry.'

'Thank you, Mr Wright,' said Sensei Terry. 'Nature provides us with precious treats. I am surrounded by these. We are connected to the Earth. We must respect the Earth. We are guests on this wonderful planet.' Focusing on Margaret, he bowed and said, 'What a big cucumber you have, madam.'

'Why, thank you, Mr Terry,' she slurred.

'Sensei,' said Sensei Terry. Not with as much force as he had earlier to Producer Neil. But still forcefully enough.

'Oh, I love a man with a strong manner,' slurred Margaret. 'Sensei Terry, thank you.' She took another gulp from her wine glass. Some of her bright red lipstick stayed on the lip of the glass.

'How did you grow such a large cucumber?' asked Sensei Terry.

'Well, I sing to them at night,' she said, and hiccupped.

'You sing to them? How lovely,' said Sensei Terry. 'What will you do with it now you've won?'

'Well, I shall be eating cucumber sandwiches for about a month,' she slurred.

'I bet,' said Sensei Terry.

'I hear you can break a brick in half with your bare hands,' she purred at Sensei Terry.

'Yes, I can. It's just my *chi* power and focusing the energy that is within all of us,' he replied.

'Would you be able to break a cucumber in half? Not *any* cucumber – but say my prize-winning super-sized one here?' asked Margaret Babble, gesturing to the green salad monster on the prize-winner's table.

'Of course I could,' said Sensei.

'Who wants Sensei Terry to karate-chop my cucumber?' asked a now woozy-looking Margaret

Babble. The entire tent started chanting in unison.

'Chop it. Chop it. Chop it, chop it!'

The crowd loved Sensei Terry. This was worrying for the competition, but even I found myself screaming at him, 'CHOP IT!!!'

'Very well – if you are very sure . . .' and on that, Sensei Terry handed his microphone to Margaret and rolled up the right-hand sleeve of his karate *gi*. He placed his left hand on the cucumber ever so lightly. Marking the spot for impact.

No sooner had the left hand been taken away, than Sensei Terry's powerful right hand came down:

CHOP!

The County Spring Fair's most Amazing Vegetable exploded with a SPLAT, showering the crowd with cucumber pulp. It would probably be very good for their skin.

People screamed; they loved it. The giant cucumber had been no match for Sensei Terry's karate chop. He was in the zone and looked ready to pounce on the rest of the innocent prize-winning vegetables on the table.

It was at that moment that Producer Neil made a big mistake. Observing proceedings from the back of the tent, he looked at his watch and realised the interview time on air was up. The next song was obviously due to start. He rushed towards Sensei Terry and reached out from behind to touch his shoulder – merely to let him know he needed to wrap up the interview.

As we know, though, you don't lay hands on Sensei Terry without good reason and NEVER without warning.

I guess because it was seconds after his karate chop, he was still in full warrior mode. The ninja postman didn't even turn round to see who had put their hand on him. Maybe he thought it was the amazing cucumber fighting back but, within nanoseconds, both of his hands had instinctively come up to Producer Neil's wrist, which he twisted sharply. At the same time he shoved his hip into the poor innocent radio producer's legs and performed what is known by Sensei Terry as a hip toss.

Over his shoulder went Producer Neil and his fall back to earth was kindly cushioned by the still wine-woozy Margaret Babble.

The tent went deathly silent as Margaret Babble lay sprawled beneath Producer Neil. A few moments of shocked silence passed and then I heard someone mutter, 'Is she dead?' and another, 'Psycho'.

Bad news for Sensei Terry and his efforts to win Radio Star. Great news for me. As for Margaret, it turned out she wasn't dead. After a moment she sat up, burped, and said, 'Does anyone have any more wine?'

I left the tent that truly had lived up to its name.

Amazing.

CHAPTER 47

My interview

'OK, Spike, the young challenger, you are up next. As the only actual DJ here, it's your job now to show everyone how it's done after the last two . . . efforts,' said Howard 'The Howie' Wright, trailing off as he realised he hadn't a clue how best to describe the chaos so far. 'As a dog owner yourself, it's man's best friend for you today. You will be interviewing, live on Kool FM, the Best in Show dog.'

'You want me to interview a *dog*?' I asked. Grandad Ray let out a sarcastic laugh.

'No! The owner, obviously,' said Howard 'The Howie' Wright.

'Struggling already, Spike,' muttered Grandad Ray. I accidentally on purpose trod on his foot.

'Owwwww! Watch it, you clumsy kid,' he yelled.

'No way to speak to a child, let alone your own grandson,' said Sensei Terry and fixed Grandad Ray with an icy stare. He massaged his left hand and a knuckle cracked loudly. It had the desired effect of silencing Grandad Ray.

'I'll take you over to the dog arena now,' said Producer Neil.

In the arena, I'd never seen so many dogs in all my life. Dogs of all shapes and sizes. Some with bows round their necks and all looking immaculate after being blow-dried at the dog hairdresser. While all the dogs were different, their owners all had something in common. Each and every one looked utterly mad. Crazy-eyed and very intense people. Producer Neil introduced me to the owner of the winning dog.

'This is the winner – Tony Storey. And this is his winning dog, Geoff.' I shook Tony's hand and wondered who calls their dog Geoff. I made a mental note to ask about the name in our interview. I looked at his winning dog, Geoff, and saw it was a pug. Pugs, to me, look like they've run at great speed face-first into a brick wall. Geoff's pug face was fixed permanently in a sneer. As if he had just smelt something really awful. How he had won, I had no idea.

'Thirty seconds till you are live, Spike – good luck,' said Producer Neil as he handed me a microphone.

I tried to control my breathing and focus myself. I saw Holly and Artie behind the barrier that ran round this arena we were in. Holly mouthed 'Good luck' at me and Artie gave me a thumbs up as he stuffed a hot cross bun into his mouth. Seeing them made me happy. Great friends can do that sometimes without even saying a word. Just by being there for you.

'Five . . . four . . . three . . . two . . . one,' counted down Producer Neil and pointed to me as he got to one.

'*Hi, it's Kool FM live from the County Fair. Howard "The Howie" Wright here, and today we find the winner of Radio Star. Our HUUUUUGGE competition to find Kool FM a brand-new DJ. We have four finalists going up against each other, but only one can win the big prize – looking after my amaaaazzzzing radio show*

for a week, trained by me. What a prize!

'We will now hear from our youngest contestant – it's Spike Hughes, also known as Radio Boy from the Secret Shed Show. I hope he can perform outside of his mum and dad's garden shed! Let's go live to him now as he does a special interview for us. Spike, are you there?'

'Thank you, Howie, yes I am. Welcome, everyone, and let me introduce you to Tony Storey. His dog has just been crowned winner of Best in Show,' I said.

'Thank you, young man. I'm not the winner really, though – Geoff here is,' he said. Geoff the pug just stared off into the distance towards the burger van parked nearby. I quickly thought of a joke.

'He's staring at that burger van. Maybe he fancies a hot dog! HOT DOG – get it?' The crowd laughed politely. After the mess of Fish Face and Sensei Terry's interviews, I was finally showing everyone some real skill. With an early laugh, the crowd were on my side. Not Grandad Ray, who I could see in the distance snarling at me.

'Now, his name, Mr Storey. Why Geoff?' I asked.

'That's a good question. Geoff was my late dad's

name and I wanted to honour him by naming my new precious pug puppy after him. He reminds me of my dad.' If I was to name an animal after my Grandad Ray, it would have to be a venomous snake.

'Did your dad have a squishy face and trouble breathing like Geoff here?' I asked.

'No. Of course he didn't. Geoff has the same colour fur as dear old Dad's hair,' said Tony Storey in a very huffy voice.

'URGGH!' I screamed. 'Geoff, NO.'

Geoff had lifted his little stumpy leg and weed on my right one. People were in stitches, laughing. This was not going well.

'I'm so sorry,' said Tony, horrified at what his prize-winning pooch had done.

Sorry? Your wheezing furball has PEED on me, I wanted to say, but I needed to regain my composure. I was live on Kool FM and my claim to winning Radio Star hung on this interview. I stank of dog wee. I could've done with some of Grandad's aftershave, that's how bad I smelled. It broke my concentration. My mind suddenly went blank. I couldn't think of a single question. *Oh no, what's happening?* Then I told myself: *just roll with it.* Like on the park bench.

'I bet you must miss your dad,' I said.

'I do,' said Tony. 'But it's hardest on my mum. They were very close.'

My mind suddenly flashed back to the park bench and chatting to old Violet.

'She must miss him terribly,' I said.

'Yes. In fact, do you know, she still goes to the park every day to sit on their favourite bench.'

I blinked. That name: Geoff. The park bench. 'Wait. Is your mum . . . Violet?'

'Yes!' said Tony. 'How do you know?'

'I met her!' I said. 'We carved her and Geoff's names

into the bench and the park warden tried to stop us but . . . um . . .'

'That was *you*?' said Tony. He grabbed my hand and pumped it up and down. 'Thank you! That made her day, you know. Her week! Her *year*! You, sir, are a remarkable young man.'

The crowd all went 'ahhh'. I was getting the cute kid treatment. Thanks, Violet.

I looked down at Geoff, the ugly pug. 'I suggested to your mum that she should get a dog,' I said. 'She said she was lonely, and dog owners always talk to each other at the park, don't they? Maybe you could help. I mean, you obviously know your dogs. You've won Best in Show!'

Tony's eyes lit up.

'That's a *great* idea,' he said. 'I could help her pick out a puppy. Something not too big . . . maybe a spaniel . . .' And he was off, working out which dog would be best.

I was back in the game now and on a roll. I saw Holly in the crowd, nodding her approval. *Nice one, Holly – your interview training was inspired and is paying off.* Near her Grandad Ray, sticking his fingers down his throat and pretending to be sick. What a sad old man. Both of them, in different ways, spurred me on. Time for a big finish.

'Well, there you go, ladies and gentlemen. A loving son who is going to find the perfect puppy for his mum for Easter. And to top it all, I have been peed on by an award-winning dog. But that's OK. It's award-winning wee, I guess,' I said.

Tony Storey laughed. Holly and Artie both gave me a thumbs up each. I even heard Howard 'The Howie' Wright giggling in my headphones.

'*Wow, what a pro! Spike Hughes there, Radio Boy, making us laugh and cry, and showing tremendous calm under pressure. That's* some *interview. He sets the gold standard for Radio Star. If he can handle Geoff the pug, he can easily do this show! BUT – there are three others who also want the big prize,*' said Howie as he played the next song. Producer Neil came over.

'That was brilliant, Howie couldn't have done it any better himself!' he said excitedly.

Over in the distant corner of the arena I spotted Grandad Snake still staring at me. He knew I'd just done the best interview of the day. If he wanted to win, he would need to beat me. TOP THAT, TOPPER!

CHAPTER 48

And then there was one

Next up was Grandad Ray. With Fish Face and Sensei Terry out of the running, it was all about Grandad. It always had been. He'd promised revenge. This was it. Him against me.

Grandad vs Grandson. The Battle of the Hugheses.

It isn't exactly normal to go into battle against your grandad, but then again Grandad Ray is not your normal grandad.

Grandad's challenge was to interview the owner of the Cow of the Year. A prize-winning cow. Was that really a thing? How does one cow look any better than another one? Not just the best cow, but COW OF THE YEAR.

We all made our way to the livestock pens where all the sheep and cows were kept. Grandad Ray took his comb out of his back pocket and fixed his hair.

Just as he walked away to start the interview, Nan suddenly appeared at my side. I hadn't seen her since she had thrown Grandad Ray out. She hugged and kissed me on the cheek. Grandad Ray looked over from the pens and his eyes grew as big as prize-winning apples. I thought they were about to pop out of his head.

'I see he hasn't changed a bit, Spike,' whispered Nan. 'I'm sorry he's behaving like this.' She looked over at Grandad Ray, who was getting ready to talk about a cow, but was struggling to concentrate, with Nan's appearance.

Finally he gave up trying and came over to see her. They walked off to the corner of an empty pen to talk, but with Producer Neil trailing after, as they were about to go live. I couldn't hear what they said, but from Nan's body language, the wagging finger and shaking of her head, she was telling her husband and my grandad off big time. She even pointed over at me a few times while giving him a well-deserved ear-bashing. Eventually, Producer Neil managed to drag Grandad back to the Cow of the Year. Grandad Ray kept looking over at Nan and I thought I saw a tear in his eye. Ruthlessly, all I could think was: how would this affect his interview and attempt to win Radio Star?

The PA system around the Spring Fair came alive again and Howard 'The Howie' Wright started to introduce the final contender. My stomach danced about with nerves and I just wished it would all be over quickly now, so I could know the outcome.

'Well, everyone, it all comes down to this final moment. A family at war. Old versus young. Let me introduce a grandad who used to be a singer under the name Toni Fandango. It's Toni Fandango versus Radio Boy. Two generations, but only one can win . . . my amazing competition: RADIO STAR.'

A big round of applause and a cheer rang out from around the fair.

'We go live now to a man who does his own show

called Ballroom Banter, *Let's see just how well he can banter about cows!'*

Producer Neil signalled to Grandad Ray that he was live. There was only the sound of silence. Seconds passed. People began to ask in whispers what was going on.

Only I knew what was happening. Grandad Ray had closed his eyes, which I knew meant only one thing. He was about to sing. He was bringing out the big guns.

Grandad Ray had summoned the spirit of Toni Fandango.

I'm building up my problems . . .'

Artie was standing next to me with Holly. 'Nicely done, Grandad Ray, that's a song by The Wonder Stuff from years ago called "The Size of a Cow",' he said. *Thanks for the support, Artie.*

The entire county show cheered as the song finally came to an end, and broke into applause. Grandad had got down on one knee to sing to the cow. The farmer loved it, the Cow of the Year loved it and so did the whole of the Spring Fair. Damn it. He was nailing this.

I could see my chances of winning Radio Star disappearing as fast as the racing ferrets I'd watched over in Ring Four earlier. That was when I spotted the thing that gave me a very bad idea.

The animals of all shapes and sizes were kept safely behind gated pens. Big cages of all sorts, each filled with the separate types of animals. From your fast little ferrets, to the woolly sheep and terrifying bulls with rings through their noses. And, of course, the cows in the pen next to Grandad Ray and the Cow of the Year.

The gates were controlled electronically. I saw some big plugs, switches and thick cables that ran to the pens. If I turned off the power to the cow pens, then they would all be on the loose. Grandad Ray's moment would surely end in disaster.

There was another switch labelled MASTER in black marker pen. Which one should I flick off? I needed to make sure *all* the cows got on the loose, not just a few of them. I guessed the MASTER switch was the one that would do that. As I heard more laughter for Grandad Ray, my mind was made up. I had to take action to stop him snatching Radio Star from me. I pushed the big red switch on the MASTER plug to OFF.

At first nothing happened and Grandad Ray happily waffled on to the delight of everyone. Where were the escaping cows? Finally, with relief, I saw that the cows had discovered their gates were open and they had begun to plod towards Grandad Ray, who remained oblivious to his imminent fate. My plan was working!

In the next moment, however, with horror, I began to see that it wasn't just the cows who had escaped their pens. Oh no, what had I done? ALL the pens for ALL the animals had opened, and now sheep, llamas, pigs, goats and cows were free. It took a while for them to realise this, but slowly the animals started to wander out of all their various enclosures and into the tents and all over the showground.

Cows kicked out at rude pigs who barged into them, goats started chewing the tent ropes, and sheep scattered in all directions as dogs began chasing them. People started running everywhere, screaming. What had I *done*?

Grandad Ray, never a brave man, threw his microphone to the ground and starting running

COUNTY SPRING FAIR

about, screeching, 'LLAMAS! HELP ME! LLAMAS!' In his bid to escape the arrogant-looking llamas closing in on him, Grandad Ray pushed a woman and child out of his way.

Who would have known my grandad was llamaphobic?

'*DON'T PANIC!*' yelled Howard 'The Howie' Wright live on Kool FM.

This was before he saw a panicked horse kick a very large dent into his new car.

CHAPTER 49

The Aftermath

It took all of the County Fair security team (what a busy day for them), and even the Army motorcycle display team, to recapture the animal escapees enjoying a free ticket, courtesy of me, to the Spring Fair ground. There was a rumour that a couple of llamas had a spin on the big wheel and a sheep boarded the helter-skelter.

Finally, calm and safety was restored to the Fair. But it looked like a hurricane had swept through the place.

My sister had found her pony, Mr Toffee, helping

himself to some candyfloss. She jumped on him and helped round up some of the animals like a cowgirl. Later that week a photo of her doing this made it into our local newspaper with the headline, 'Amber to the rescue!'

There was a television news helicopter buzzing around above us, showing the chaos to its viewers. This wasn't the first time something I had done had made the teatime news. At least when it was the school strike about homework, I was the unknown Radio Boy.

Would I be able to keep what I'd done this time a secret?

The answer was: no.

Artie and Holly found me hiding behind the Kool FM broadcast van.

'Did you do something to cause this, Spike?' said Holly quietly. She could see from my state of wide-eyed fear that I had, plus she was another one with ninja mind-reading powers. In fact she made my dad look like a complete amateur.

I silently nodded my head. I was so frightened by what I'd done, words failed me.

'They think it was an electrical fault that caused

all the gates to open – and unless you want to be disqualified from Radio Star, you should make sure they don't know any different,' said Holly.

'Five policemen are still chasing one pig that's going berserk in the cake tent. It's been drinking the chocolate fountain and is having a sugar rush,' laughed Artie. At least he was having fun.

Howard 'The Howie' Wright turned up at the van, looking red-faced and stressed. Producer Neil was behind him as always. Both smelled of several kinds of animal poo. I think I caught the perfume of llama droppings in there, with just a hint of cowpat and subtle undertones of pig splats.

'My new sports car has been vandalised by a rampaging horse!' blurted out The Howie. I thought he was going to cry. The worst damage had been done to his driver's door, where the slogan 'This car is driven by Howard "The Howie" Wright, star of Kool FM' was plastered all down the side. Why would anyone want people to know who was driving the car? Did it mean other drivers gave way to him in traffic?

If *that* works, why don't more people paint slogans on their cars, saying what job they do? 'This car is driven by Doctor Norris!' Doctor Norris is our family doctor and a nice man. People would always let him out of a junction if they knew it was him in the car. Not sure about Mr Kundy at Number 57, though. He's an estate agent.

'It's OK, everyone, I'll call the dealership showroom tomorrow to get it all repaired,' Producer Neil reassured The Howie. No one was particularly interested, however.

'We need to announce the winner of Radio Star so we can all get out of this hellhole,' declared Howard 'The Howie' Wright. He then turned to Producer Neil and said, 'We are NEVER coming back here again.'

Producer Neil patted his back, like a parent might do to an upset kid who'd just accidentally let go of his balloon.

We were all instructed to follow Howie to the backstage area. We were in varying states of emotion. Grandad Ray had eventually been calmed by one of the Spring Fair first-aiders. He was rocking back and forth on a hay bale, wrapped in a blanket, talking to himself.

Sensei Terry was in usual Zen-like calm mood, despite the misfortune of Margaret Babble and

Producer Neil. Mr Harris was holding an ice pack to the side of his face where the prize-winning salted-caramel cake had struck.

'Come this way to the main stage,' urged Producer Neil.

'Please, let's go crown the winner of Radio Star,' said Howie.

It was time.

CHAPTER 50

And the winner is...

All the Radio Star contestants, and the Kool FM team, weaved our way through the utter carnage the 'electrical wipe-out' had caused, towards the stage where the competition winner would finally be announced. It really did look like a tornado had swept through the place. Stalls of wood carvings and candles had been knocked over and there was straw everywhere. I genuinely felt bad, but if I won this competition, it would be worth it. Luckily no one had been injured or hurt, had they? And were a dented car and some broken wood carvings really much to worry about?

Mum and Dad joined the procession of people heading towards the main stage. Mum put her arm round me and kissed me gently on the head. 'You're my winner, always,' she said. Normally I'd shrug this off and say, 'Mum, I'm not a baby any more,' but it was welcome this time. I needed it.

Dad, the original mind-reading ninja, whispered as we walked along.

'I have a feeling that electrical meltdown may not have been an accident, Spike. Just a hunch. I saw you lurking around the main power area, you see, and then, as if by magic . . . All I'll say once again, is: choices, son, choices. Be true to who you really are and be careful you don't lose sight of that.' He patted me on the shoulder and jerked a thumb at Grandad Ray. 'Don't go to the dark side.'

Dad moved away, taking Mum with him. His words bounced around in my head, much as I wanted them to go away.

We got to the foot of the County Fair main stage.

It was a large covered outdoor stage, and to me it seemed huge. Big enough for a band to play on. There was quite a crowd waiting there, despite the events of the last hour and the animal break-out.

Producer Neil gathered us all round him. 'We are going to go to the side of the main stage. Howie will chat to the crowd and update everyone listening on Kool FM, then bring you all out. He will then announce the winner.' He looked at everyone to check we'd understood.

'Good afternoon, everyone here at the Spring Fair!' shouted Howie. He got a decent cheer, but after all the crowd had had a pretty difficult time. What with all that running for your life from stampeding cattle.

'Well, um . . . after the electrical problems and every animal here accidentally being let out, everything is now OK. No one got hurt, which is good news. Let's hear it for the fantastic security here today and the Army motorcycle display team . . .' This got a bigger cheer. 'On stage now and live on Kool FM we are going to announce the winner of Radio Star! Please welcome our finalists . . .' said Howie.

As we walked out on to the main stage, the crowd

gave us all a warm round of applause.

'Drum roll, please, Neil,' instructed Howie. Now back in his element, controlling the show. Producer Neil played the sound effect of a drum roll; my stomach churned. Grandad Ray got out his comb and readjusted his quiff. Sensei Terry, still in his immaculately white karate *gi*, closed his eyes and breathed slowly.

Mr Harris adjusted his tie.

'It has been an incredible grand final here on Kool FM at the County Fair. Our finalists have given us some truly memorable radio. Let's look back at what's happened here today . . .'

Howie then played a recap of all of our final challenges. Starting with me and the dog peeing on me. Hearing my interview back, it wasn't as bad as I thought. Then it was into Mr Harris meeting a former pupil whose school life he wrecked and who sought revenge through his award-winning-cake attack.

Sensei Terry next, and just hearing the pandemonium of Producer Neil being mistaken for an attacker and hurled through the air on to Margaret Babble was hilarious. Awesome.

Then came my nemesis, Grandad Ray, singing again

as Howie played back his moment. You could clearly hear the crowd loving it and him, until again we heard him screaming 'Llama! Llama!' and running away. I couldn't help but laugh. He glared at me. He looked right into me; he knew I was responsible. I looked away.

'. . . and the winner of Kool FM's Radio Star is . . .

'It's Radio Boy himself . . . step forward, SPIKE HUGHES.'

I'D WON! GOODBYE, SHED, HELLO, SHOWBIZ!

CHAPTER 51

Decisions, decisions

'YESSSS!' I yelled like I'd never yelled before. I could hardly breathe with the exhilaration of it all. I was a winner and Grandad Ray was the loser.

Howard 'The Howie' Wright handed me a microphone.

'This is incredible! Er . . . thanks. I've won! I'm Radio Boy and I AM A RADIO STAR!'

The crowd cheered. This felt great. So this was what it felt like to be a winner. I took it all in. Finally now

YESSS! I was officially a celebrity DJ. No more smelly, cold, cobwebbed garden shed for me! Photos were immediately taken of me with a huge grin holding the Radio Star trophy. Once the official photographer was done, I was ushered away by the great Howard 'The Howie' Wright.

'This is all yours, Spike,' he said, waving at the crowd. 'You are the future.'

'Can't wait to get in your proper studio with Artie and Holly,' I said. 'They will love all the equipment and the chance to broadcast to the whole county!'

'Oh, don't you go worrying about them, Spike, you won't need them any more. Neil will be producing you instead of a child amateur, and we'll get you a proper professional sidekick, not some cake-eating machine.'

I looked over at Artie and Holly, who were cheering

for me. Artie was finishing off an ice cream the size of his head. They looked so happy for me.

Dad's words echoed in my mind.

Be true to who you really are.

I thought about Holly, scared in the supply cupboard. How supportive she'd been to me.

'*Trust your instincts*,' she'd said earlier.

I thought about Artie. My sidekick, my wingman. How lucky I was to have them. How much they had helped me win.

I realised I hadn't even thanked Artie and Holly on stage and now Howie was asking me to just drop them and I had actually considered it for a moment. Without them I would have nothing.

What was I *doing*?

I caught my dad's eye and he smiled. The ninja mind-reader was at it again. There might come a time in my life when I would certainly *not* want my dad reading my mind. I didn't care today, though. He knew what I was thinking because it was the only right thing to do.

I grabbed a microphone and asked Producer Neil if I could say a last few words.

'Sure, it's your moment, why not?' he said and ushered me back on stage.

'Well, our winner here has a few more words he wants to say,' yelled Howie, 'and as he is the Radio Star, he can do what he wants; back to you, Spike – I mean, Radio Boy.'

I stood on the stage staring out at the crowd, and at first words failed me. It was eerily quiet in the showground, as most of the people were standing in front of me waiting to hear what I had to say. Even the sheep had stopped bleating and the cows mooing.

I swallowed nervously, and looked at the trophy in my hand.

'I cannot accept this,' I said into the mic.

CHAPTER 52

Choices

'I cannot accept this,' I repeated.

I was terrified, but strengthened by knowing I was doing the right thing. I said it again, but louder and more sure this time.

'What are you talking about, Spike? Sure you can!' joked Howie nervously.

'No, I can't, Howard.'

'Please – to you, it's The Howie,' he said generously.

'Thanks. But this prize isn't for me.'

The strange hush in the crowd ended and people were now talking, trying to understand what on earth was happening. It had certainly been a day of the unexpected at the Spring Fair this year.

'It was me,' I said. 'It was me that caused the "electrical meltdown" during my grandad's interview challenge. I was jealous about how well my Grandad Ray was doing and I wanted to win so much. Too much.'

'YOU NAUGHTY BOY!' yelled some lady in the background. I looked around and saw it was my mum. Dad started to try and calm her down.

'I thought winning was everything, but actually I was losing so much. I'm not a Radio Star, but I *am* Radio Boy.'

I handed Howie my microphone and walked off the stage. Dad was first to find me, and he hugged me. At that moment, he obviously wasn't thinking about the enormous bill he was going to get for the dry-cleaning from a crowd covered in straw and cowpats.

'Choices, Dad, choices,' I said to him.

Sensei Terry came over and said wisely, 'Sometimes, Spike, in life, it isn't the path you walk down, it's the path you don't walk down.' For once, I knew exactly what he meant.

Artie and Holly came running over to me.

'You are full of surprises, Spike Hughes,' Holly said. 'Turning off the electrics and causing chaos! But then saying no to that prize – that took real bravery. You wanted it so much.'

'I thought I did. Part of me thinks I must be mad turning it down,' I said.

'I don't,' said Holly.

'I very much DO,' said Artie.

'You don't get it,' I said. 'They weren't going to let you two come with me. It would have been me and Producer Neil filling in for The Howie's holiday.'

A pause.

'Oh,' said Artie.

'And you turned it down . . . because of us?' said Holly.

'Well, partly,' I said.

She gave me a quick hug, and for a moment I felt that strange warm feeling I'd felt when we touched in the store cupboard. Then she pulled away and grinned. 'Right, I'm going to go and get a hot cross bun,' she said.

'And I'm going to get some music,' said Artie. And then headed over to a stall selling second-hand records.

I looked over at the Radio Star trophy (an oversized golden microphone) that was now lying unwanted on the stage floor. Geoff, the award-winning peeing pug I'd met before, went up to it and did what he'd done earlier to my leg.

Exactly, Geoff.

CHAPTER 53

And the winner is...

So now there was a Radio Star vacancy. Who would be standing where I'd been only a few minutes ago, receiving the trophy?

We soon found out. Howard 'The Howie' Wright was back on stage. Producer Neil was applying some disinfectant to the Radio Star trophy.

'Well, today just keeps getting more interesting . . . So, we now have a new winner. And it's yet another member of the Hughes broadcasting dynasty . . . The new winner of Radio Star is Grandad Ray!' The crowd cheered its approval.

While I knew I had made the right decision, this was going to be awful. Grandad Ray would be unbearable.

He walked past me and I braced myself for how pleased with himself he would be up there.

Grandad took the microphone that Howie offered him and paused. I saw that right at the front, behind the metal barrier, was Nan. Grandad Ray saw her too and he froze. I mean he just stood there, looking at her. It was like he was seeing her for the first time. His face softened.

Howie broke the silence. 'Obviously in some shock, old fella, but maybe we can get a song or something from you to sum up how you feel about winning this amazing prize?' he suggested.

This was actually a good idea as Grandad Ray certainly preferred to let songs do the talking for him.

He struck his trademark wide-legged pose.

'S-s-s-since my BABY left meeeee . . .'

Artie later told me this was an old Elvis Presley song called 'Heartbreak Hotel'. When performed/ strangled by Grandad, it was more 'Heartbreak Bed and Breakfast'.

He then fell dramatically to one knee. Something clicked as he did and Grandad Ray grimaced.

'Wow! I get the feeling you're speaking to someone special here today, Ray,' said Howie.

Grandad Ray leaped back up – maybe too quickly, as I heard another bone make an awful crunching noise.

'Yes, I've been a fool. I did all this for you, Diane. I wanted to show you I could do something. Please take me back, I'm
sorry. I can change . . .'

I could see Nan looking at him and thinking, 'Can this man really change?'

Grandad Ray saw this too. 'I *can* change. Diane, I honestly can . . . Mr Howard Howie Wright, I can't accept this award, right though it is to give it to me as I was the best.' Grandad Ray shot a look my way. He just couldn't help himself.

He then looked back at Nan, who was shaking her head. Grandad Ray saw his chance at a reunion slipping away.

'I can change! I have gone too far and upset my grandson. But it isn't worth all this. I just entered this Radio Star thingy to get my own back about being sacked from his radio show. I am sorry, Spike. I don't blame him totally, it's that bossy girl Holly – no offence, Holly.'

Holly shook her head at Grandad.

And then it was time for another song from Grandad Ray, back to one of his favourites.

'What becommmmmmmesss of the broken-hearrrrrtted . . .'

It was enough for Nan Diane. While he crooned his song to her, she clambered over the crash barrier, assisted by Sensei Terry, and on to the stage where she and Grandad Ray hugged. Producer Neil burst into tears. I'm not sure if it was the sight of two old people still in love or the fact that they now had yet another problem with this competition.

Two people had now turned down Radio Star live

on air. What were they going to do now?

The Howie didn't look very happy.

'How can this day get any worse? I know what we'll do! The winner, the most honourable man here, the Radio Star, is Sensei Terry!'

The crowd managed another cheer, despite being a bit cheered-out by now.

Well, thank goodness he hadn't given it to Fish Face! I was happy with my black-belt postman getting my job. *Good choice, Howie.*

Sensei Terry bowed and struck a karate pose. Howie shoved a microphone into his face and probably prayed yet another person wouldn't resign.

'Thank you, everyone. The real winner today isn't me – this is all about love. Love yourself, your friends, your life,' said Sensei Terry to rapturous applause from the now very emotional crowd. He bowed.

'Bor-ring!' came a familiar voice at the back. It was Mr Harris as he stormed off the stage.

At that moment his son Martin marched to the front of the stage and grabbed Howie's microphone. What on earth was happening now?

'Dad, I quit. I don't want to be part of your dumb

radio show,' said the son of Fish Face. Martin Harris, in a day of many twists and turns, had given us another shock.

Good for him, I thought.

It must be a nightmare having a dad like that. My feelings of sympathy subsided a bit when I saw Katherine Hamilton run up and put her arms round him.

He wasn't the only one getting some special attention. The newly crowned winner of Radio Star, Sensei Terry, was also the focus of affection. From the lady he'd flattened earlier by throwing Producer Neil on top of her. Margaret Babble, with a fresh goldfish-bowl-sized glass of wine, was draped all over Sensei Terry. He appeared to have red lipstick on the collar of his *gi*.

I had nothing.

That's not true. I had my shed studio. I had Artie and Holly. I had *me* back.

I had everything.

CHAPTER 54

the Final Chapter

I opened the rickety shed door at the bottom of the garden of Number 27 Crow Crescent. The door has been warped by decades of sun and rain, so takes quite some effort to open it. Once I'd summoned the strength of ten men, I entered my shabby, dirty, dusty, smelly studio. I felt at home.

Sure, it's no comparison to what I could've had at Kool FM. Air-conditioning, my own butler/producer in Neil and probably my own car with my name on it eventually. But this was home.

Maybe one day I'll have a studio like that for real. Maybe I don't need to rush there just yet. Looking at my mum and dad sometimes, I think being a grown-up is overrated. I turned on all the equipment, accidentally kicking over a plant pot in the process. It was obviously home to a million and one creepy-crawlies that were now on the loose. This was their home too and I really didn't mind. I turned my mic on and the big MIC LIVE sign glowed red.

'Hey, Radio Boy here. I've had quite a day today. Can I be honest with you? I've been a bit of an idiot. I thought I wanted something very much and actually I didn't. I thought it would make me happy, but I've learned the hard way today that no prize, or trophy or fame, can do that. Well, maybe it can for a bit, but it won't last because it's not real. I spent so much time trying to win, thinking that if I did I would be happier, that I forgot to be happy with what I already have. I stopped noticing all the good stuff I have in my life. This, here, in this shack of a shed, *this* is my happy.'

The shed door opened and the person entering saluted me. I carried on talking.

'I'd like to play a song now, but someone's going to sing this one live. It's my Grandad Ray. Today, let's call him Toni Fandango.'

With that Grandad Ray, the great Toni Fandango, sang, with all his being. The shed window rattled, such was the power of his booming voice. Loud and over the top. It was perfect.

'Weeeeeeee arreee family,' he sang, so loudly that a can of paint fell off a shelf, maybe in a desperate attempt to take its own life. Who knows?

I invited Grandad to stick around on the show, but he declined and headed out of the shed door, where I could see Nan waiting for him. His beaten-up fake snakeskin suitcases were there too. He was finally moving out and going back to Nan, where he belonged.

He paused for a second and came back in and up to the microphone. He placed his hands on the desk and leaned in. I guessed he wanted to say a final apology to me and how much he really loved me.

'We both know I would've won that competition if you hadn't pulled that plug and set them beasts loose on me,' he said.

We stared at each other. A deadlock. Sherlock growled at Grandad Ray. Nan came in and asked, 'Everything OK in here?' 'Sure, just telling my grandson how special he is,' Grandad lied. He smiled at me.

I smiled back. He's possibly the world's worst grandad. But he's never boring or dull.

'See you, Toni Fandango,' I said.

With that he turned and left, but not before he'd pulled my favourite ice cream out of his cool bag and handed it to me. He winked and said, 'You're the biggest star in this family, kid.'

CHAPTER 55

One last thing

It was pouring with rain so Dad was giving me a lift to school.

'Can I turn the radio on?' I asked.

'Sure,' said Dad.

I tuned to Kool FM as I did every morning to hear Howard 'The Howie' Wright's show.

'Hi, this is Sensei Terry, on Kool FM, looking after Howie's show while he's on holiday, in some exotic place no doubt.* Anyway, after the news, our new

---

* There was in fact some doubt that he was in the Caribbean, as Mum swore she saw Howard 'The Howie' Wright with his mum at the local caravan park. When I asked if it was definitely him, she said she was very sure as his horse-dented car with his name on it was there.

feature, "Can Sensei Terry break it?" This morning I'll be attempting to karate-chop a brick, an iPhone and a front door. My producer, Morning Margaret,* will be assisting.'

I smiled to myself. Sensei Terry was doing a great job. I thought I might have been jealous hearing him doing Howie's show, but I wasn't. How could I be? On *my* show tonight we were holding a competition to do the best impression of your parents, and the big prize was one of Glenn Tims's award-winning cakes.

If it was good enough for Mr Harris's face, it was good enough for my listeners.

* Morning Margaret was Sensei Terry's news producer on his show, supervised by Producer Neil. Morning Margaret was Margaret Babble.

Note from me, the writer of this, Spike Hughes

Thanks for buying my second Radio Boy book. The fact so many people bought the first means this book exists, so thank you. It also means Katherine Harris has to start noticing me now I have TWO books out.

The cash I get from this book will go on:

- Some new headphones. Mine were cheap ones Mum got from the market and appear to be made of dust and air. They are as strong as really old underpants when they lose their elasticness. And smell as bad.
- A treat for Sherlock. One of those fake shoes from the pet shop that dogs love and chew for days.
- Some decent aftershave for Grandad Ray.

Thanks for reading. I feel like we are in a secret gang. You can let anyone you want into that gang by telling them about this book. And if you'd like to drop me a line, do: radioboy@radioboy.co.uk

I gotta go. It's show time and this radio show isn't going to present itself. Be awesome.

Radio Boy AKA Spike Hughes

Acknowledgements

It's a ghastly word that. Who even says, 'Can I just acknowledge you?', or 'acknowledge you' instead of 'thank you'?

I'm not sure what's a better word or phrase. I asked my kids, which is what I've done whenever I got stuck with this book, and they said 'fist bumps'. I'll go with that, then. So join me as I fist bump the following people:

My wife, Sarah. For pushing me when I was having a meltdown. For daring to say you can do better. Being there to bounce ideas off and, annoyingly, having better ideas. Now go and write your own book. No really. Do. You helped the writer in me; now I'm returning the favour.

My two mini editors, Ruby and Lois. The fact-checkers of this book. Hearing you both roar with laughter was always what I was aiming for. Thanks for taking the time to read all the early drafts, or being kind enough to lie and say you had and that they were great. Big love, your loyal dad servant.

Sean Hughes. RIP. You aren't around on this planet to thank in person, and I did when you were, but I have to say this here anyway. I gave Spike your surname. When I was younger, you had a big impact on me and I hope Spike can do the same for someone like me who feels a little lost. Sometimes laughing at serious things makes them seem a little bit less scary.

Rob Biddulph, the genius illustrator. Spinning my half-baked ideas into gold. If you can do such a thing, he did it.

Nick Lake, my guru and patient editor, who basically took a sprawling book so big and long it would've taken a young reader through childhood, adolescence and into early retirement before finishing it, then examined each line like a master jeweller with an eye glass, before stepping back and working out how to find more gems and lose the flab.

The brilliant team at HarperCollins: Elorine Grant, text designer; Kate Clarke, cover designer; Samantha Stewart, desk editor; Tanya Hougham, the slave-driving audio editor; and the entire Sales, Marketing and PR team for helping me no doubt take home a Pulitzer with this very book.

To all the Radio Boy fans who have sent emails, posted reviews and helped spread the word: only the smartest kids get this book. The other fools read you-know-who and what's-his-face. Not you. The future is safe in your gifted hands. Thank you from this slightly older Radio Boy.

Marks & Spencer's Madagascan Vanilla Fudge. My treat at the end of each chapter.